BRUTAL MATE

PLANET OF KINGS BOOK 1

LEE SAVINO &
TABITHA BLACK

SILVERWOOD PRESS

This book is a work of fiction. The names, characters, places, and incidents are products of the writers' imagination or have been used fictitiously and are not to be construed as real. Any resemblance to persons, living or dead, actual events, locales or organizations is entirely coincidental.

This book contains descriptions of many sexual practices, but this is a work of fiction and, as such, should not be used in any way as a guide. The author and publisher will not be responsible for any loss, harm, injury, or death resulting from use of the information contained within. In other words, don't try this at home, folks!

BRUTAL MATE

One minute I'm walking back home from a nightclub. The next, I'm waking up in a cage.

Abducted by aliens. Given to an alien race. Put up for auction. But instead of being sold to the highest bidder, I'm rescued by one of the Brutal Ones: the biggest, baddest bullies in the universe.

But it's not a rescue. Not really. My rescuer makes it clear he wants something in return for saving my life...

... an Omega.

Me.

ONE

Emma

"It has to be on there. Please look again." I hate the plaintive note in my voice but at this stage, it's impossible not to whine.

The bouncer's bushy eyebrows almost meet in the middle as he stares first at his clipboard, then at me. "Sorry," he says gruffly. "There's no Emma Turpin listed here."

That fucker! He promised! A gust of wind threatens to lift my miniscule skirt and I frantically pin it down over my butt with one hand, clutching my bag with the other. "James Macklemoore. He said he'd get me on the list. Do you know him? He told me to come here tonight—"

"If you're not on the list," the bouncer leans forward, his growing impatience obvious, "you're not on the list. So you don't get in. Invitation only." Raising his big head, giving me a good view of his broad, blotchy neck, he addresses the woman behind me. "Next!"

"Wh-what am I supposed to do now?" I bleat.

Returning his attention to me even as the lady behind

me gives a huff of impatience, the bouncer shrugs his huge shoulders. "Go home?" he suggests.

Spectacularly unhelpful.

Finally admitting defeat, I swallow a pithy remark and step out of the line, moving aside to let the next hopeful be vetted for entry. The building which houses the latest and most happenin' BDSM club this side of Richmond doesn't look like much from the outside, but it's grown so popular in such a short amount of time that capacity is limited, and it's now the kind of place you can only get into if you know someone.

Which is why I danced circles of delight when my friend Susan told me she'd met a guy who could get us in.

A guy who had obviously been lying.

I take a few steps away from the bouncers, the velvet rope, and the queue of would-be club guests. I need a moment to think, to mull over my options.

A chilly breeze cuts across my path, and I shiver as I wobble down the shadowy sidewalk. I'm wearing heels more suited to the bedroom than for walking in, a skirt so short I don't dare bend over in it for fear of indecent exposure, and a halter neck top which emphasizes my boobs quite nicely, but doesn't offer anything in the way of warmth or comfort.

It's nine in the evening. I grit my teeth against the cold —I'm already covered in goosebumps.

And I don't have my car.

I'd been hoping to get off with someone at the club. In order to do that, I would have needed some liquid courage, and therefore I had decided to get a lift instead of driving myself. A friend of mine offered to drop me off here on her way to work—she's a waitress at another club downtown.

It had never even occurred to me that I might get turned away at the door. Susan is one of my best friends, and she doesn't usually hang out with what we refer to as *bad types*—liars, cheaters, and so on. She had asked me to wait until she had an evening off too, so we could go together, but I, Little Miss Impatient, had to refuse that suggestion, didn't I? Instead, I asked her to get the mysterious James to make sure my name was on the list for Friday night.

That has obviously not happened.

Dammit.

Fishing my phone out of my little clutch purse, I finger it for a moment, debating my next move. All dressed up with nowhere to go. Do I head home, admitting defeat? Do I try another club?

Another brisk gust of wind whips around my bare thighs, and my ensuing shiver almost makes me double over. Fuck this. I'm going home.

I could call an Uber, but I don't live that far away, and it might be a good idea to walk off some of the frustration I'm currently trying to keep a lid on. There's even a shortcut if I go through a couple of fields.

Glancing back at the queue, I see the woman who was behind me has disappeared, apparently having been permitted entry into the hallowed halls of *Retribution*. She's probably sipping her first drink and enjoying the warmth of being indoors. Perhaps she's even already being chatted up by some tall, handsome Dom who's promising to do all sorts of delicious things to her.

Meanwhile, my nose is starting to run from the cold. I turn and begin the trek back to my apartment.

This is just all so typical. Why me? Why do these things always happen to me?

It's been six months since Dane and I broke up and, heartbroken over losing the man I had loved and been with for over a year, I had thrown myself into my work, deliberately not thinking about dating, or sex, or BDSM, or anything for which an attractive male partner is required.

Until stupid ass Susan told me about this stupid ass club and that stupid ass James guy, and all my previously buried desires came flooding back to the point where I thought I'd go nuts if I didn't feel someone's arms around me again.

Or their hand on my butt.

Or their tongue on my....

Having reached the first field, I pause to take off my high heels, shuddering at the freezing ground beneath my bare feet. *When I get home*, I vow furiously, *I'm going to get into my warm, fluffy unicorn onesie and make myself the biggest mug of hot chocolate, with loads of cream and maybe even sprinkles.*

Do I have sprinkles at home?

It doesn't matter. Even without toppings, there's something inherently comforting about hot cocoa. Especially when you combine it with cookies.

One benefit to breaking up with someone and having your heart torn to shreds is the inevitable loss of appetite, which inevitably leads to weight loss. For me, anyway. I know others deal with it differently, seeking comfort in food, but I was never one of those women. Still, years of being on the pill added some twenty pounds to my frame, and one upshot of all this crap is that most of that has now dropped off again.

Otherwise, I wouldn't have been able to get into this outfit.

If I wasn't feeling so sorry for myself, I'd be laughing at my current situation. Once I'm home and no longer having my legs whipped by reedy stalks instead of a hunky Dom, I might already see the funny side to all this. But at this moment in time, I'm throwing myself a massive pity party, and my misery only grows when I lurch off balance with a *squelch*. There's a thick, gross slurping sensation around my bare foot. I've stepped right into a patch of black mud.

Fucking great.

It's too dark, I can barely see where I'm going, and there's no way I can discern enough on the ground to be able to navigate around it, so I decide to go all in and take another step into the cold, slimy gloop.

Mud is meant to be good for the skin, anyway, right? Don't they do mud facials at spas?

The going is slower now that my feet are being sucked into the ground with every step, and I'm praying the stuff is actually mud, and not some kind of animal poop. That would just be horrendous.

Then again, no animal on this Earth would crap quite so extensively—unless an entire herd decided to use the same spot in which to defecate. I'm walking and walking, and getting more and more tired, and there still doesn't seem to be any end in sight.

In fact, as I look around, the whole landscape around me seems to be shifting—growing blacker, more ominous, more oppressive.

Here, close to a big city, the sky is usually relatively light even at night but that, too, seems to have darkened.

What the capital eff is going on?

I stop still in my tracks, clutching my purse as if for comfort, my bare feet slowly sinking into the cold, viscous mud, and look around, trying to get my bearings.

Everything around me is just getting darker and darker. Like I'm being suffocated with a huge, wet, black blanket.

Out of nowhere, as if it's just remembered it needs to react to this new state of fear, my heart begins to pound madly, and my throat feels like it's closing up.

Great. Now I'm having a panic attack.

With trembling fingers, I scramble to get my phone out

of my purse. Am I imagining things, or am I feeling the mud around my *ankles* now? I look down for confirmation.

Yep. I'm definitely sinking.

Sinking into the mud.

Fuck this! Too terrified to even curse out loud, I toss my phone back into the bag, yank my feet free of the gloop, and take off running.

Or at least, I try. Stumbling is a more accurate description as I drag my heels through the mud, doing a weird reverse kind of Moonwalk, my heart crashing against my ribcage.

It's getting darker and darker, as if a giant, silent fist is closing around me. I'm not making any forward progress. But what will happen if I stop fighting?

My purse still in one hand, my shoes in the other, I claw the thickening air, slipping and sliding in the general direction of home. My body is numb. The long grass slashes at my bare legs, the wind whips through my hair—but I feel nothing. Reality is slipping away, leaving only this suffocating black nothingness, enveloping me in a dark, dense fog.

I can't escape.

My last coherent thought, as I start turning in squelchy circles, my chest heaving in terror, is: *what the actual capital fuck is happening to me?*

Then... nothing.

TWO

Emma

SHARDS OF GLASS are piercing my skull. I squeeze my eyes shut against the pain. I draw in a deep breath and splutter. The air is like mud—thick, viscous, stinking. Like I fell asleep in a dumpster—but worse.

Where in the name of coffee am I?

With extreme reluctance, purposefully taking shallower breaths and trying to ignore the crackling headache, I lift my eyelids.

I'm dreaming—well, having a nightmare. Hallucinating, that's it. There's no way this is reality.

It can't be.

I'm in a cage. An actual cage. Gloomy light reflects off the bars. The metal mesh under me cuts into my bare butt. I shift, and more spikes of pain stab my head. My eyes water as I press a hand to my forehead and whimper.

The stench of this strange place is like a wretched, damp cloth covering my face. I wave my hand in front of my nose, my movements slow. My arms ache like I've done a hundred push-ups. My stomach doesn't feel too great either.

Remembering I always have some meds in my bag, I look for it. It's nowhere to be seen. Nor are my shoes. I must have lost both on the way here. Fuck.

I grasp the bars, gagging and panting. And freeze.

I'm not alone. Surrounding me are forms that could never be called human beings. Creatures? Aliens? Figments of my imagination, in any case. They're grunting to one another in a language I couldn't hope to pronounce, let alone understand, and I press a trembling hand to my mouth to stifle the scream that's threatening to burst from me.

This isn't happening. I'm just having a terrible, vivid nightmare. In a minute, I'll wake up and find myself in my soft, fluffy bed.

After all, this is real life. There's no way I'm really in a cage, apparently being guarded by a half dozen things that look like what you'd get if King Kong had mated with a T-rex.

Well over eight feet tall, they have huge bodies and glistening, flat snouts. Thick black fur covers their torsos and arms, while their lower halves look more... lizardly, with scales and thick, long, blunt tails. Their arms are quite short, but their fingers are tipped with claws.

I've never seen anything so terrifying. Not even on a movie screen.

I suck in another deep breath, and let out a cough-splutter-whimper. Damn this weird alien air. There's a fist around my lungs, squeezing. I can't get enough oxygen.

Great. I'm going to suffocate in a bizarre nightmare.

The creatures must have heard my noise. As one, they all turn their heads to regard me, cocking them to the side like birds.

I stare back. My imagination is pretty impressive if it

can come up with so much detail in a dream. The creatures move with fluid grace, tails twitching behind them.

One of them grunts something to another. The second one heads to a table in the corner and returns holding, joy of joys, an enormous syringe.

I hate needles. Loathe and detest them. And that's when they're being administered by a trained, professional human in a medical setting for my own health—not when a supersize one is being brandished at me by a horrifying alien creature while I'm trapped in a cage.

My panic—already at a level previously unknown to me—kicks up another notch.

"No!" I scream, rattling the bars of the cage in a pathetic attempt to... do what, exactly? Bend them or rip them out so I can escape? Scare these huge creatures? "No, please don't stick that in me, please... I'll do anything... I just want to go home."

An enormous, talon-tipped hand grips my upper arm and yanks me up against the bars. The creature's strength is undeniable. If it decides not to let me go, I'm not going anywhere...

My bare toes, still caked with dried mud, are scrabbling at the cold stone floor as the syringe is aimed at my neck.

Hang on a second. My neck?

"You are not sticking that thing in my neck!" I say with as much authority as I can muster. "Forget it. Not. Going. To. Happen."

The thing grunts, I feel a sharp prick in the sensitive spot beneath my right ear, and then, for the second time in what I assume is the same evening, everything goes dark.

THIS TIME, when I awaken, the needling pain in my skull has faded to a dull ache, and I can suck in air more easily. It still smells musty and weird, but I don't choke every time I try to fill my lungs.

The side of my neck is throbbing, and I'm curled up in a little ball in the corner of the cage. The weird lizard-gorilla creatures are still there, talking amongst themselves in hushed, grunting tones.

"...wake up soon..."

"... that she arrived here just in time for the auction..."

"...hope the translator chip will recognize her native tongue, and function..."

"...so small and fragile, sure they won't break her?"

"...be starting soon, hope she wakes in time..."

I'm exhausted, scared out of my wits, and confused as fuck, so it takes me a moment to realize that I can actually understand what they're saying. How? Some weird alien technology? Does it have anything to do with what they injected into me?

My fingertip finds the spot on my neck where the needle went in and I prod it, wincing. There's a tiny lump just below the surface of the skin. A chip? Have these fuckers actually *microchipped* me?

Or am I still dreaming, and really imagining all this?

Swallowing past my dry throat, I take another musty breath and call out, "Hey! You!"

Instantly they hush and, as one, just like last time, they all turn their heads to peer at me.

"You awake," one of them grunts, taking a step closer to my cage.

"No thanks to you." *Easy, Emma, don't antagonize them.*

"No... thanks?" Another of the aliens tilts his head,

contemplating my statement. So they seem to understand what I'm saying. Sort of.

"It means... oh, never mind." I sigh. "Which one of you is the leader?"

"Leader?" The word the creature uses is a guttural exclamation but I still understand him perfectly. So strange.

"Yes. Who's in charge? Captain? Chief? Boss? You know, the head honcho."

They all look at one another in turn. Then one whispers something. He has a blue scar over his eyebrow. "Me," he says, in a tone of disbelief.

I get the impression there is no hierarchy here, and they're just pretending for my sake. I don't care. I'm going to get home, one way or another. That's my only objective. "Okay, you'll do," I say to Blue Scar in as sweet a tone as I can muster. "I think there's been some kind of a mistake. I'm not meant to be here. I don't want any harm to come to you —ideally, I don't want any more harm to come to *myself*, either—so how about you just let me out of this cage and show me how to get home?"

He comes closer and his gaze meets mine. His eyes are round and dark, deep pools with swirls of silver. Hypnotic. I blink and look away. "No," he says at length. "You stay here. You go to auction. You good for Ulfarri, or other bidders."

Wait—what? I'm not sure I heard him correctly. "Auction?" I say slowly.

"Yes. Girl slaves. You go into heat soon, good for Alphas to mate. Alphas pay well for good mate."

I take a moment to absorb this absurdity. *So let me get this straight. In the course of one Friday evening, I've been denied entry to a kink club, turned away at the door, then fallen through a mud-slick wormhole into another dimension? Galaxy? Something alien, anyway. Then I was locked in a cage, injected with god-knows-what against my will (although we've already established it's some kind of microchip and translation software), and now they're going to auction me off as a sex slave to something called an Alpha?*

Yeah... that's not gonna happen.

Ever.

Then another part of his statement penetrates the confused haze of my racing brain.

"Wait a second. Did you say I'll be *going into heat* soon?" I ask, astounded at how calm and rational my voice sounds even as I can't believe I'm having this conversation at all.

Blue Scar nods. "You go into estrus and crazy for Alpha. Make Alpha crazy for you. You will mate. You will breed."

"Oh will I, indeed?" My left eyebrow is so far up my forehead at this point that it must almost be touching my hairline. "I don't think so... what's your name? Are you Ulfarri?"

This makes the other creatures let out a series of croaks, a hideous, guttural laughter. At least, I assume what they're displaying is mirth.

Blue Scar shakes his head. "We Ogsul, not Ulfarri. Ulfarri are Brutal Ones. Everyone afraid of Ulfarri. But don't worry. They kind to their mates."

"Of course they are," I mutter under my breath. "They're not *human* males."

Even if that tiny bit of snark went right over the assembled creatures' heads, I find some comfort in the fact that despite this horrific situation, I'm still holding on to my sense of humor.

Frankly, at this point, I don't seem to have a whole lot else.

"But not just Ulfarri at auction," Blue Scar continues.

"Others too. Highest bidder will win. Perhaps you lucky. Perhaps you not get taken by Ulfarri."

"Ulfarri mate lots," grunts another of the creatures. *Yay. Commentary from the peanut gallery.* I bite back a sigh as he continues. "Go through many females. Take sex slaves. Wear them out."

"I see." My voice actually has a note of boredom in it. I'm on overload. I can't take any of this seriously. If I do, I'll freak out. And I don't have the energy for a full freakout. This is all so absurd and such light years away from reality that it can't possibly be true. Or even actually happening.

Certain that I'll be waking up at any minute, I feel free to let my inner brat shine through. These things have apparently kidnapped me. I can't fight, but I can bitch at them.

Not that it seems to bother them much. More's the pity.

I shift into a crouch and my top flops down, exposing more of my breast. I try to cover up but my club clothes are torn, filthy and generally completely ruined. "Do you have anything else for me to wear?" I ask Blue Scar. "Who would want to bid on me if I'm dressed like this?" Not that I want anyone to bid on me, but I want to know what he will say.

Blue Scar shrugs. "Bidders don't care about... clothing." His mouth gapes open in what must be the most hideous smile in the known universe, revealing weird, square teeth. "Don't worry. You be naked very, very soon." His stinking breath hits my face, and my rose-colored glasses shatter.

I clutch at my ruined top, my stomach lurching. "What?"

"Yes." Blue Scar nods. "You wait, Omega."

Omega?

"I don't know what you're talking about." I force the words out around the rocks in my throat. "There's been some sort of mistake. I'm human."

"Yes. Hoo-man. And now Omega. Made to fuck." He gestures at my body. I realize I'm trembling.

What?

"You go into estrus soon. Alpha scent you. Mate you. Knot you."

Not me? What does he mean? "That's not, I'm not..." I'm stammering.

"You are, now. Omega." Blue Scar leers at me, but I can't bring myself to ask any more questions. I slap my hand over my mouth. If I puke now, I'll have to wear it. Not that there's anything in my stomach.

I just want to be in bed, at home, alone. "Wake up, Emma," I mutter. "Please, please wake up."

There's a terrible grating noise of metal screeching over metal, and I jerk around. One of the other creatures is unlocking the cage.

"It's time, Omega," Blue Scar says, his long teeth flashing in the low light. "You go to auction."

THREE

Khan

Spaceports always have a potent stench—the result of so many species crammed into a small space. I hold my breath against the stale reek of recycled air as I navigate the dark corridors on my way from my ship to the dark cantina. Only after I've settled at a table do I adjust my hood and take a careful inhale. The jumble of scents isn't always unpleasant. There are just so many smells all at once. No wonder my fellow Alphas prefer our home planet to space travel.

Today, the air is flavored with a thick musk from the Ogsul, the reptilian species running the auction. There are a million of them slinking around this spaceport. There's a hint of sulfur from a Buruwr, a giant, gelatinous creature sitting in its own trail of slime right in front of the auction stage. But underneath the overwhelming cacophony of smells, there's a delicate scent. Fragrant. Floral. Slightly musky.

The cantina is full of alien creatures, but no sign of what could produce such an amazing aroma. The perfume is growing stronger, like someone filled the room with a bouquet of blooms. But it's not a flower; it's a female. There are rumors of a special female to be found on the spaceport. That's why I'm here.

The stool creaks under me as I shift my weight. A few creatures glance my way and snap their gazes from mine. No one wants to catch the attention of an Ulfarri Alpha.

I rap the dinky table and, after a minute, a reluctant Ogsul trudges across the room with a drink for me.

"Brutal One." The Ogsul bows and leaves the smoking vat of my preferred fermented drink on the table beside me. I sniff but don't touch the oily liquid.

"Wait," I growl. A tremble runs up from his scaled tail to his hairy shoulders, but the Ogsul stops. "Tell me about the auction."

A pause. I don't have to negotiate or threaten. As an Alpha, my reputation precedes me. They call us the Brutal Ones for a reason.

"Sorry," the Ogsul says. "I get my chief." And he scurries away.

I settle back on the stool. The honey scent is growing heavier, sweeter. My canines ache, and my own rich scent is growing stronger in response.

Maybe the rumors are true. Maybe my travels across the galaxies have finally met with success. Maybe the time has come for me to find what I've been searching for all my life, what any Alpha would kill for: an Omega.

"Brutal One." Another Ogsul, this one taller with bulging eyes, appears at my table. He doesn't tremble but stands rigid, several lengths away. I beckon, and he takes a small step closer.

Close enough. I lean forward, keeping my face in shadow and my voice low. "Do you have the female?"

The thick black hair on his arms rises. "We have many females. For auction." His stumpy arm motions to the stage.

"But the..." If I say the word *Omega*, it's as good as shouting. "I heard you have something I want," I murmur.

Ahead and to my right, the giant, slug-like Buruwr quivers, more bitter-smelling goo leaking from it onto the floor. Creatures across the universe will pay to plant their seed in the Omega's fragrant, sacred womb. If the Buruwr wins the bid, it will take what is mine.

It will not win. I slide my hand down to stroke the hidden curve of my scimitar.

"There are tales that you have found what I am seeking. I am here, and I am willing to pay."

The creature's throat vibrates, a bitter scent pouring off his shaggy and scaly hide. But when I set a bag of coins on the table, his eyes bulge bigger.

"Yes," the Ogsul says, bobbing his head. "An Omega."

"You have one?" I forget myself and growl. The Ogsul leaps backwards a length faster than such a bulky creature should move. I curl my fist around my scimitar handle. "Where is the Omega? Tell me, now." I've searched long and far for a female to adequately replace the Omegas of my kind. So far, no luck.

"We prepare her. Auction."

"Is she Ulfarri?"

"No, Brutal One."

Damn. Probably some cow-titted creature. But a womb is a womb. And I want heirs.

"We have serum," he squeaks. "There is a creature we found that can take the Omega serum."

Interesting. I must learn more about this serum. But first... "Describe this creature."

"It called *Hoo-man.*" The Ogsul pulls out a holopad, and shows me a shadowy image. Not much to be seen but a small, frightened face surrounded by a mass of golden hair, peering out between the bars of a cage. Pale skin peeks out between shredded clothing.

"Frail," I sneer. "That will not satisfy me." I don't know this for sure. I won't know until I'm in a room with her. And if she is an Omega...

"It sentient," the Ogsul tells me. He takes a step forward, apparently overcoming his fear in his eagerness to make a sale. "Pretty. It won't disappoint."

"Fine." I feign boredom. "Show me."

The Ogsul's throat works up and down before he answers. "Auction soon."

I growl again, and the low murmur in the cantina is sucked away. "I do not wish to attend an auction," I say into the silence.

"Many creatures here to see the Hoo-man."

Hoo-man. I curl my tongue around the foreign word. This is another dead end. "Very well." I wave a hand, and the Ogsul bows and keeps bowing as he backs away. Like I've granted him a favor. Which I have. Maybe I won't kill anyone today.

My throat vibrates with a low growl. My hand tightens on the handle of my blade. I pride myself on my control, but there's one situation where even an Alpha struggles to keep control: the rut. When we're in heat, when we scent a sweet little Omega in the vicinity, even the most powerful Alphas are mindless.

And I'm as powerful as they come. I've fucked females of every size, shape, and species, and enjoyed most, but there's one type which has eluded me until now.

The sacred Omega.

My fated mate. The one female I was born to fuck.

Could this Hoo-man really be an Omega?

I lick my lips. The perfumed scent is thicker now.

Still delicate and sweet, but growing in intensity. Is this the Hoo-man? My cock is awake, throbbing in my breeches.

The cantina is near packed now. Creatures stand between the tables, facing the stage. They've come to gawk over the pretty slaves of all different species, fitted with translation chips which will allow them to understand and speak any of the known languages, regardless of their own origin.

The Ogsul are a strange lot, but they do hold a good auction. I heard rumors they had a serum that could produce Omegas, but only now has that been verified. The last of the Omegas disappeared on Ulfaria a generation ago. If I can find one... I can breed her.

The Hoo-man was a pale, frail looking thing in the picture, but if she produces such perfume, I will buy her. And if anyone tries to bid higher, I will show them why my species, the Ulfarri, are called the Brutal Ones.

Perhaps this night will be more promising than I thought.

Getting to my feet, I take to the shadows, leaning back against the wall, crossing my arms. I'm tall enough to see easily over the heads of the other assembled males in the room. A wide variety of species have come to purchase a female, judging by the stinking males crowding this cantina. The small, cruel Rheeza, with their horned skulls and pointed noses. The docile, almost painfully shy Alags, with their four arms and purple skin. In the corner hunches a rare Haggat. So pale as to almost be translucent, his blazing third eye flicks back and forth over the assembled crowd of males, all of whom are apparently desperate for an Omega female.

They're all weaklings compared to me. Compared to the Alpha. I already pity the females they'll purchase. The one I choose—should I find the Hoo-man worthy—should be grateful she's escaped a much worse fate.

There's a screech, then a crackle, and then one of the Ogsul plods onto the stage. He's holding a microphone and looking enormously pleased with himself.

"Gentlemen, thank you for traveling such long way," he begins in his thick, guttural language. He seems to have a much broader vocabulary than most of the Ogsul I've met before. "As always, we have a fine array of females for you to choose from, so please be generous in your bids." He hesitates, then hums and leans forward. "I'm especially pleased to be able to tell you that we have one of the rarest kinds of females on offer for you tonight." He pauses for effect again before continuing. "An Omega."

There's a hum of excitement traveling around the room, and I know that every other male is thinking the same thing I am:

That Omega will be mine.

The noxious stench in the room thickens as the dozens of males lean forward, eager to get a glimpse of the first female slave for sale. I duck my head further in my hood to gain a little reprieve from the blend of sweat and testosterone. No trace of the sweet floral scent from earlier, the perfect honey scent like light on my tongue. Curse my sensitive sense of smell. I should have brought a breathing mask. Thank Ulf I'm not in rut, else I'd be gagging by now.

"First female on offer is number 327, a shy little Tyreen!"

There's a deep rumble of lowered voices as the obviously petrified slave is shoved unceremoniously onstage. She has thick black hair falling in waves down to her knees, her dress is torn, and all six of her nipples are clearly visible through the sheer fabric. I can almost sense her trembling from my position at the back of the room.

Leaning forward, I inhale deeply, concentrating in order to separate her scent from the other smells in the room. There's definitely an underlying trace of sweetness, but it doesn't stir me. I lean back and fold my arms once more.

A female with six breasts and pale lilac skin will always garner attention from some males, and there are a flurry of bids being roared from one end of the room to the other. At length, the Tyreen is sold to a great beast of a Dajok, who has difficulty hiding his smug grin as he strides toward the stage to claim his new slave.

One after another, females of all kinds are led onto the wooden platform, all of them in various states of undress. Some look petrified, others look mutinous. But they're all sold, regardless. There is no escape. That is the way of the universe.

I fondle the handle of my scimitar. It's been ages, and there's still no sign of the promised Hoo-man. The stench of so many species crammed into a small space is thick enough to cut. I still have plenty of competition. Only the wealthiest and most powerful would stand a chance at winning her, so the males of lesser species are contenting themselves with the other goods on offer. Most of them have already collected their new purchases and left, so I have a clear overview of the males I must beat in order to make the rare jewel mine.

"And now, saving the best for last, I'm proud to present the promised Omega! A Hoo-man!" the Ogsul host announces.

As the evening's highlight is propelled onstage, the remaining males lean forward as one, myself included.

So, this is a Hoo-man. She's smaller than I anticipated—a lot smaller. Pale pink skin, two arms, two legs, two breasts. But the cloud of tousled hair around her head is a glittering gold, her eyes are huge and innocent and, when her rich, honeyed perfume hits my nostrils, I bite back a roar as the rut grips me with no warning; no preamble.

Suddenly, my cock is rock solid and pounding, my skin prickles, and my pulse is thudding in my ears.

I'm no longer able to form a coherent thought. My entire being screams just one thing:

She will be mine.

FOUR

Emma

For what feels like an eternity, I've been guarded in the wings just offstage behind a rudimentary curtain, waiting for my turn as female after female was forced out to be ogled and sold like cattle at market. The weird alien creatures have me surrounded, and there's no hope of escape. Besides, where would I go? It's not like I could run outside and hop on a bus, or call an Uber.

For all I know, I'm on a spaceship. Or another planet.

And I still can't believe I'm even entertaining that notion. My head hurts just thinking about it. When am I going to wake up? Pinching myself hasn't helped, though, so for now all I can do is stand here and wait my turn, trying unsuccessfully to tamp down the panic which keeps threatening to burst out of me in a scream.

Am I really about to be sold as a sex slave?

To an *alien*?

The people—sorry, creatures—bidding on the females are a loud, raucous bunch but I haven't been able to get the tiniest glimpse of them from where I'm standing. I'm not sure whether that's a good or a bad thing. I can certainly smell them, though—a thick, heavy scent reminiscent of old socks and mothballs. My mouth is filled with a bitter taste.

Judging by the variety of shapes and sizes of females I've witnessed being shoved onstage, there's no telling what the males will look like. The first slave who got sold had six breasts.

Who will purchase me? Maybe I'll get lucky and snag someone with a conscience or a kind heart, who will take pity on me when he realizes I'm not actually meant to be here, and help me get home.

Please don't let it be an Alpha. Anyone but the Ulfarri my captors were talking about, the sex-crazed brutes who wear out females at an alarming rate. All I wanted was a fun night out. Now I'm shivering in the rags of my clothes, praying I don't get shagged to death.

My headache has receded but my skin is flushed, feverish. Chills grip me, alternating with fiery flashes of heat. My stomach is cramping. Whether I'm sick from the stench of the alien air, from fear, from the stuff the Ogsul shot me up with... it's anyone's guess.

Suddenly, my upper arm is gripped by one of the creatures guarding me, and my heart jumps into my throat as I'm propelled to the middle of the stage. Bright lights blind me and I blink rapidly, trying desperately to see the audience. I hear the announcer say something about a human, and my knees turn to water. I'm only still on my feet because one of my captors is still holding me up.

This is the worst nightmare I've ever had, or will ever have. And it's beyond time to wake the fuck up.

Slowly, I'm able to make out shapes in the dark room beyond. The place is packed with dozens of alien creatures —some with feathers, some with snouts, some which look like they're made of blades—and they're shouting over one another, leaping up and down, gesticulating to the point where the host is struggling to keep up with the bidding. The place sounds like a barnyard. There's no earthly equivalent to the inhuman shrieks and groans.

It smells like a barnyard, too. The stench is making me gag. I double over, trying to cover my chest with my arms, but my bicep is still in a vice grip. I breathe through my mouth, feeling sick and feverish, and stare down at the stage, trying to pretend this isn't happening.

But it is.

Beside me, the Ogsul auctioneer is shouting. He reaches over with a stubby arm and grips my chin, forcing my face up. Again, the stench hits me. I blink against it, wavering on my feet. I would fall but for the bruising shackle of my Ogsul captor's hand.

The auctioneer points to a giant slug-like thing quivering up near the front of the stage. Have I just been sold to Jabba the Hut? The aliens crowding the stage cackle and shriek.

I duck my head but get no relief. The noise, the cacophony of alien colors and shapes, swirl into one. My skin is boiling hot. I pant for air, but a scent is rising from me now in waves, sickly sweet. I can't breathe.

A deep, primal roar reverberates around the room, drowning out everything else. The sound is like thunder, sending lightning bolts of sensation flashing down my spine. I rear back, unable to flee because of the Ogsul gripping me. My stomach cramps again.

In the shadows at the back of the room, a storm is brewing. A feathered alien goes flying with a squawk. Both my captor and the auctioneer stare. Then another shape comes flying up on stage, and drops with a splat at the auctioneer's feet. An awful alien head gapes at us, its mouth lolling open, green goo leaking from the severed neck.

The auctioneer screams and throws himself off stage. Beyond the bodies packed at the front, a huge, terrifying figure is making its way toward us, plowing through the other males like a tornado through a trailer park.

And a scent rises, thick and juicy and nothing like the stench before. It's a clean rain in the desert. A billowing, thunderstorm smell washing over me, cutting through the stale, sweaty stench, and turning the air sweet. A sweetness that turns into a rich, almost chocolatey flavor that tingles on my tongue. The taste twists my fear into something new, something unexpected. Warmth coils in my core.

The scent is coming from the hooded warrior across the room. I squint, trying to see better despite my pounding heart, and then wish I hadn't. He's a giant shadow specter in a dark hood, his silver blade flashing in front of him like Death's scythe. Creatures scramble out of his way. Too slow, and their bodies meet the deadly storm of steel. They're sliced apart, limbs flying outwards, their howls of anguish and surrender rising above the general commotion.

It's terrifying. I should run. But I'm trapped in the clutches of an Ogsul. Held doubly captive by the creature and the delicious, drenching scent.

"Ulfarri. Alpha," the Ogsul clutching me mutters, and lets go of my arm to scramble away. And I'm left alone on stage, facing the Alpha with only the huge, quivering Jabba the Hut-like creature between us.

Out flashes the curving swath of metal. The warrior's sword, wielded with expert force. It blurs and cleaves the Jabba the Hut blob. The blob... bursts. Fluid explodes through the room, searing the air with a gaseous, sulfuric smell. Aliens are shrieking, trying to get away, slipping on the remains of the fallen. The warrior in the cowl flicks his sword, casually beheading a few more creatures as they pass. Then there's no one in his path. Nothing between me and the murdering monolith. Black eyes glitter in his dark hood.

He's looking straight at me.

A terror unlike any I've ever known takes over my entire being and I'm no longer able to think. Acting on pure instinct, taking advantage of the fact that I'm no longer being held in place, I spin on my heels and run blindly, shoving my way past the auction host and racing back toward the narrow door that leads to the room I was held in before. There must be a way out of here. There *has* to be.

I cannot let the Brutal One get me. I just can't.

Strong hands grasp my waist, and I'm falling. I'm off balance, being lifted into the air. I don't need to look to know what's happening.

He's got me.

The Alpha.

This is the alien I heard whispers about after I got the chip and was able to understand my captors. One sentence keeps echoing through my mind, over and over again.

Ulfarri are Brutal Ones.

The scream I've been holding in ever since this nightmare began—which already feels like an eternity—bursts out of me, and is swiftly muffled by a huge, hot palm being slapped across my mouth.

I scream anyway. I scream until there is not an ounce of air left in my lungs, and then I sag, exhausted, dangling limply in the Ulfarri's hold.

My lips are tingling. In fact, my whole body is tingling. My eyes are closed, and have been since he caught me mid-run, so afraid am I of what I'll see. What he'll look like up close.

Some things are better if they remain unknown.

But my other senses are still there, and they seem strangely heightened. I can taste his skin, as his hand is still pressed against my mouth. His thick arm threads around my midsection, crushing me against him. He must be immensely strong to lift me with just one arm, as his other hand is muzzling me despite the fact I've stopped screaming into it.

But it's the smell that has the greatest effect on me. Musky, masculine, with a slightly sweet overtone, it's like a combination of all my favorite scents: rich chocolate, smoky bonfires, cinnamon spice. His fresh scent clashes with the stale air. Everything else smells wrong. He smells right. The fresh cologne fills me as if it were a solid thing, seeping into my every pore and setting my entire body alight with—

Lust.

The most potent, desperate desire I have ever felt clenches me. My body knots with cramps—not in my stomach, but lower down. My womb aches. My mouth is literally watering. The thudding between my thighs is matched by the frantic beating of my heart. There's a prickle between my legs, and hot liquid seeps into the sexy little thong I put on in anticipation of playing at the club.

What the absolute fuck is going on?

The Ulfarri is shifting me in his arms, turning me around to face him, and then he speaks for the first time. His voice is like a knife scraping over stone as he says a single word.

"Mine."

Forcing myself to take shallower breaths, trying to breathe through my mouth instead of my nose in case the heavenly smell surrounding me is indeed what's making me soak my thong and desperate to grind myself up against the nearest available surface, I make myself open my eyes and look at the male who currently has me imprisoned against his huge, hard body.

With his hood thrown back, he looks similar to a human

man, aside from his unusual coloring. His eyes are dark, glittering pools, he has a straight, aquiline nose, and a wide mouth framed by a neat beard. A long, thick mane of midnight blue hair tumbles over his broad shoulders.

Shrouded by his cloak, his chest bears faint markings, like tiger stripes on his pale lilac skin. They look like tattoos. I can't see much of the rest of him, crushed against him as I am, but I can feel his rippling muscles and unquestionable strength.

In slow motion, he lifts his head and his nostrils flare. He's... scenting me. Do I smell as good to him as he does to me? The decadent, chocolatey scent envelops me. There's a hint of fresh coffee too. *Mmm.*

A growl tears from the Alpha, and my body convulses in answer, like I'm reacting to the growl. My inner muscles quiver, liquid dripping from my sex. I shift helplessly, achingly aware of the enormous erection I can feel against my thigh. Even though a prickle of terror travels up my spine at the sheer size of his cock, a bolt of lust shoots through my lower belly and my pussy spasms so hard, I gasp against his palm.

"*Hoo-man,*" he says again, his chest rumbling. "Omega. Mine." Then everything goes dark.

FIVE

Emma

It's strange, I've never fainted once in all my twenty-five years, and now I've done it three times in a row.

Then again, I guess being transported to another planet, getting chipped, and injected, then put on stage to be auctioned as a sex slave—not to mention then being captured by a creature whose delicious scent turns me into a ball of slavering lust—could all be considered fair enough reasons to black out.

It's starting to feel a bit like déjà vu as I open my eyes and blink rapidly. Where on Earth—or rather, *not* on Earth—have I ended up this time?

For a nanosecond, I hope I'm actually home and back in my bed and that all this really was the most vivid, insane nightmare I've ever had, but that hope is quickly quashed when my eyes focus enough for me to be able to take in my surroundings.

The air smells fresher. A wild, piney scent mixed with that rich coffee and chocolate perfume that clung to the Alpha's skin. His tattooed, pale purple skin. Each breath brings a fresh wave of the mouthwatering scent. Who would have thought I'd be so turned on by an alien? And not just any alien—a *Brutal One*. Now I'm surrounded by his scent. Either this is his lair, or he must be nearby. I'm surrounded by gleaming, blinding silver—the walls, the floor, the ceiling, everywhere—and there are no windows.

Is this a spaceship? Or am I still near the auction house? My first captors mentioned a space port. But this doesn't smell anything like that reeking place. This smells like the Alpha. Maybe this place belongs to him.

I shouldn't be comforted by that thought, but I am. I'm a tiny bit less freaked out, although that's not saying much. This place is still foreign and strange and scary as all get out. And it's not home.

I shift on the padded bench. I'm curled under a black blanket that's light but kept me warm. It's soft, and bears the scent of my new captor.

Sitting up slowly so I don't get dizzy, I let the blanket fall away. And then I see him. The Alpha. *The Brutal One.*

He's sitting in a large metallic stool, his large, tattooed hands resting on his knees. His midnight hair streams over his shoulder. He's watching me.

For a moment we just stare at each other, the scent of him thickening until my thighs clench. My bladder complains as I move.

Everything the Ogsul told me about Alphas falls away in light of my pressing need. I put a hand over my heart to stop it from pounding out of my chest. *I can do this. I can face him.* I clear my throat. How do I ask for a bathroom in alien?

"Um," I begin. *Good start.*

He rises off the stool, stepping closer to the bench. He's enormous—easily seven feet, with broad shoulders that couldn't fit through a standard sized door. He's wearing dark, loose pants and no shirt—just some leather straps, one of which ends at his hip with the sheath to his sword. He has mostly humanoid musculature, except no man on Earth has that many muscles. With the pale purple shade to his skin and the dark slashes of his stripe-like tattoos, he's an amazing sight. "Hoo-man," he says.

"Emma." I squint up at him. Are we going to have to communicate in monosyllables? I meet his dark eyes. His delicious scent makes me a little dizzy.

I don't know why I want to communicate with him, but I do. Those Ogsul things were able to form complete—albeit basic—sentences. I'll give it a shot.

"My name is Emma," I clarify, clearing my throat a few times so my voice doesn't come out raspy. "What's your name?"

"I am called..." The rest of the reply he gives is a series of noises I have no hope of ever being able to pronounce. In fact, my translation chip doesn't bother attempting to repeat it.

"Oh," I mutter. "I'm sorry. I don't think I can actually say that."

The corner of his wide mouth lifts. He's finding this amusing. "Not many can," he says. "Call me Khan. You can say *Khan*?"

"Khan," I repeat obediently, like a child. "Okay."

He's hovering above me impatiently, as if he's waiting for something.

"I..." I begin. Do Ulfarri have bathrooms? Similar bodily functions and requirements to humans? "I need to pee."

He looks puzzled.

Shit.

"Urinate?" I try. "Bathroom? Go potty?" I slide off the padded bench I woke up on and do my best *wee wee dance*, complete with pained, desperate expression.

Khan lets out a cross between a guffaw and a snort, and I feel my face get hot. "Make waste," he says. "Over there." He points to a door, and I'm off like a shot. To my immense relief, he makes no move to stop me.

The alien bathroom is fairly small, but luckily the facilities are pretty straightforward. It's not until I pull my tiny thong down that I see how soaked it is, and remember the hot throbbing sensation in my sex when I was in Khan's arms. I'm still embarrassed about my attempt to explain my need to pee, and my cheeks get even hotter when I remember how absolutely desperate with lust I was before I fainted. It was like the basest, most biological instinct—one I had no control over. Maybe I was out cold long enough that whatever was in that serum has worn off by now, as the urge is no longer nearly as strong, thank god.

I relieve myself, then run my hands under the tap. There's no mirror, and I'm not sure whether that's a good thing. After the evening I've had, it probably is.

This whole situation is too bizarre for words.

After a couple of deep, calming breaths to collect myself, I push my shoulders back, lift my chin, and march as confidently as I can back into the room where Khan is still standing by the bench.

"Emma," he says softly, and his voice feels like a caress. "Come to me."

I don't want to, I have no reason to, and yet my feet begin to move towards him, regardless. Does he have me under some kind of hypnotic spell?

Jesus, this all sucks so much!

Within moments, I'm standing in front of him, and what he does next startles me. Reaching out with lightning quick reflexes, he tugs me into his arms, pressing me up against his huge chest. "Breathe," he whispers, and again my body obeys his command without any conscious effort on my part. In fact, I'm not sure I'm even physically able to resist.

The heat radiating off him engulfs me, and his thick scent is even more overpowering. It's like he flipped a switch and brought me back to the lust-filled Emma I was before I fainted. An intense, slow pulse thumps between my thighs, and my heart begins to thud. I'm suddenly overwhelmed by the most insistent need I've ever experienced, and it's so all-encompassing that I'm debilitated, powerless to resist as Khan's big hand slides up the back of my neck to the base of my skull. He grips my hair, tugs my head back, and then, with a growl which vibrates through my core, he covers my mouth with his own.

He tastes as good as he smells. Rich and chocolatey, with a smokey edge.

I kiss him back with a hunger I can't fathom, gasping as his tongue finds mine and explores it with slow, passionate strokes. He's still gripping the back of my head but his other hand slides possessively down my body, exploring, kneading first my breast, then my side, then running down my hip before slipping between my legs.

When he cups my pussy in his huge palm, my swollen clit pulses against his hand, and I bite his lower lip, desperate for more of his touch. More of him.

The fever's back, a heat billowing through me with every heartbeat. Nothing else exists, nothing else matters. Khan's hands burn on my skin but if he stops touching me, my heart will stop.

I bite him again, harder, and his reaction is immediate: he tears off my panties with a single, sharp tug, then plunges two fingers deep inside me.

I'm so wet that they glide in easily, and my sex clenches around them even as he kisses me again—more roughly this time. His tongue is fucking my mouth in tandem with his fingers inside me, and my brain short circuits. I want his cock.

I *need* his cock.

He adds a third finger, stretching me. It's brutal—and I love it. I want this pleasure edged in pain. Like chocolate sprinkled with sea salt. Only when his twisting fingers fill me enough to hurt will the sensation be enough.

His thumb finds my clit and at the first stroke, I explode, a bolt of desire shooting through my lower belly as I climax, my pussy clutching rhythmically at his fingers.

He drinks my moans, coaxing wave after wave of pleasure from me, until the spasms finally abate.

Even though I've just had the hardest orgasm of my life, I mourn the loss as his fingers leave my drenched pussy and he stops kissing me. I feel empty, desperate, unsatisfied.

Like I'm in heat.

It's then that I remember the aliens' conversation. *Estrus.* That's what they called it. Going into heat. Something to do with scent. I scoffed inwardly at the idea when they mentioned it.

I'm not scoffing now. This shit is real.

Khan's eyes are fixed on mine. They're blazing with the same hunger I'm sure is reflected in my own gaze as he moves slowly, down, down... until he's on his knees. Before I can realize what's happening, he's hooked one of my legs over his broad shoulder, and his tongue is swiping along my crease.

I clutch his head, my fingers threading through his long, dark hair as he licks my clit with breathtaking precision, instinctively knowing the ideal pressure and rhythm to drive me out of my ever-loving mind.

I'm so wet, I can feel it running down the inside of my

thigh, and yet, instead of feeling ashamed that he's having this effect on me, even that sensation is turning me on more.

My entire pussy is vibrating. Khan is growling as he eats me out. It's almost like a big cat's purr, and it's doing things to me I can't explain.

All I can do is feel.

I've been on the edge of another orgasm since the moment his tongue found my aching, pulsating little nub, and it's like he's keeping me there deliberately—no surcease, no completion, just the never-ending torment of being on the razor's edge of coming.

"Please," I croak, clutching his head. I'm vaguely aware that I'm trembling. "Please..."

If he heard me, he's ignoring my pleas. Instead, he keeps on licking me, his tongue tracing circles around my engorged clit before dipping into my dripping core, gathering more of my juice before returning to the bundle of nerves my entire being has been reduced to.

I'm sobbing helplessly, grinding my hips and pulling him closer to me in a desperate attempt to find completion.

His response is to slide his hands up to my hips and grip them so hard it hurts, pinning me in place, leaving me powerless to do anything but accept the torment.

He's still growling.

I lose track of time. I lose all sense of everything but the way he's drinking from my slick core and cruelly keeping me on the edge of orgasm but not letting me go over. Every time I think I'm there, every time the first wave begins to tingle in my most sensitive spot, he redirects his attention to my entrance, thrusting his tongue inside me as far as it will go, until I want to scream—not from pleasure, but from frustration. Only once the sharp initial tingles have subsided does he return to my clit—and begin the torture all over again.

At length, I do what any normal, red-blooded girl in heat would do.

I snap.

Letting out a tortured howl, I yank his long, midnight blue hair as hard as I can, then try to kick him in the back with the leg that's hooked over his shoulder.

Khan's reaction is immediate. One big paw slides up from my hip to grip me by the throat, stunning me into immobile silence. Then, in one fluid movement, he shakes my thigh off his shoulder, rises to his feet, undoes his pants, cups my ass with his free hand, and lifts me until I'm impaled on his huge, rigid cock.

I've never known anything like it.

I didn't get a look at his member but it's easily the biggest thing I've ever had inside me. Even though I'm soaked and slippery, my pussy burns as Khan's dick plunges deep, stretching me to the point of pain, his hand around my throat making me feel light-headed with a combination of terror and arousal. I can still breathe, but I'm definitely not going anywhere.

To my astonishment and shame, I'm coming before he's even fully seated. I didn't even know I could climax from penetration alone. Unable to suppress a strangled cry of pleasure, I close my eyes so I don't have to see the way he's looking at me as my hopelessly full pussy flutters around his cock.

And he hasn't even started fucking me yet.

"Look at me," he orders in a rough whisper, and I find myself obeying even though I don't want to open my eyes, don't want to see him witness my humiliation as I continue to climax and gush all over him. He's not even moving; he's just holding me in place as I writhe and sob, impaled on his rock hard dick. It's so big, I'm whimpering, even as he hums an encouraging sound to soothe me. Then he growls and my body convulses—a dam breaking, and fluid gushing from my body to ease his passage. My inner walls clench around him in the most delicious way.

Every sensation is amplified a thousand fold. It hurts so good.

Even as I'm coming, I'm aware of the most minute details: the way the pulse in my throat is pounding against his hold. The way his scent seems to have filled my every pore. The way he's looking at me. The way his cock seems to be growing even bigger inside me.

Khan begins to move, then, thrusting his hips, fucking me slowly at first but soon gaining in pace as he, finally, seems to lose control himself...

SIX

Khan

INTOXICATING. All my life, I've heard other Alphas talk about the rut, about what happens when they catch the right Omega's perfect perfume, about the loss of control, and all-encompassing need to dominate. To claim. To fuck.

None of the descriptions even came close to portraying the reality.

Emma's honey scent permeates my being, awakening a lust within me that I never even thought possible. It's a primal urge to mate, to slake my hunger on her soft little body, to mark her as mine.

I'm so hard, it hurts.

The desire was there the first moment I caught her perfume but I held back, unwilling to frighten her, not wanting to move too quickly for fear of harming her. It would have been too easy to take her while she was unconscious, and I considered it, but this Hoo-man is going to be my mate for life.

I didn't want to ruin everything from the start.

Only when she had awakened sufficiently and returned

to me after her ablutions did I give in to the need burning inside me.

When the taste of her slick hit my tongue, I lost all ability to think rationally. Furious with her for creating such sensations in me, I tormented her deliberately, keeping her on the edge until she lost her temper.

It was adorable.

As if this little slip of a girl could do anything to stop me from taking what is now mine.

She has no choice, and we both know it.

I'm not sure when I started growling but at some point, I was aware I was doing so. It only heightened her reaction to me, making her sweet little pussy gush more slick for me to taste.

Unable to hold back any longer, I lifted her onto my pounding erection. Even though her thighs were wet with her desire, even though she was beyond aroused and on the verge of her second climax, her pussy was an incredibly tight fit, gripping my cock like a second skin as I stretched her.

I hold her in place, seated fully inside her, watching her writhe and sob as she comes undone without me even moving. Her feet aren't touching the ground; she's held aloft only by my steely grip, and my iron-hard cock.

I want this moment to last for the rest of my life.

But then the velvet fluttering around my rigid length subsides, and I'm overcome with the urge to move. I begin to thrust, slowly at first, relishing every ridge, every square inch of her as she squeezes me.

Emma was made for me. Made for this.

I thank Ulf for my stalwart control as I battle against the rut, against the need to fuck her as hard as I want to. I don't want to break her, and the size difference between us is significant. She feels so little, so fragile in my arms.

She closes her eyes, obviously lost in sensation, and I order her to open them once more. I want to drown in those blue depths, want to see every nuance of desire she has for me.

I want to see her come again, to feel her tight heat clutching around me like a pounding heart.

At the same time, a prickling sensation begins in my balls and lower belly, spreading until it's taken over my entire body, and at the point where Emma and I are joined, the knot begins to form.

The little breathy gasps she's been giving turn into moans and, slipping the hand on her throat around to the back of her neck, I yank her face to mine, suddenly desperate to kiss her again. I thrust harder, fucking her in earnest now, crushing my lips over hers and mimicking my cock's movements with my tongue against her own. Her honey taste is everything.

Her fingernails are digging into my shoulders and, just like when she bit my lip before, the sharp pain excites and infuriates me at the same time. Without conscious thought, I deliver a hard slap to her ass, the sound of which makes my ears ring.

To my astonishment, I feel her cunt gush and contract, and she lets out a low moan of pure pleasure.

Could it be that she enjoys pain?

To test that theory, I slap her again, even harder, and her reaction is unmistakable.

And it's then that I finally allow the last tether on my control to snap, and for sheer instinct to take over.

It's raw. It's primal. It's animalistic. Every nerve ending in my body is ablaze; my entire focus is narrowed down to one thing: the sweet, hot Omega who's now joined to me not just physically, but on an elemental level.

Her gasps have taken on a new tone and she's shaking in

my arms, her long lashes fluttering as she closes her eyes. She might be coming again; she might be moaning because I'm gripping her so hard that I'm hurting her—truth be told, I'm too far gone to care. The roar begins in my gut at the same time as my own climax heralds its arrival.

The knot at the base of my cock has expanded fully now, making it impossible to thrust any deeper. I'm sealed into Emma's cunt and even so, I'm still trying to fuck her, hammering my pelvis against hers as my balls tighten and I come.

Acting on sheer instinct, I lower my head and bite, sinking my teeth into the soft skin where her throat meets her shoulder. Her scream heightens the sensations in my cock as it pulsates inside her, filling her up, every jolt adding more seed to her overflowing pussy until the ecstasy finally begins to abate, and I slow my movements to an eventual stop.

I feel like I'm waking slowly from a dream.

My groin and upper thighs are soaked with our mingled juices—her slick and my cum are seeping out of her even around the seal formed by the knot.

Emma is trembling in my arms and I slide them around her, holding her close, burying my nose in her silky golden hair, willing her to calm. To settle.

She's silent but her shoulders are shaking. Is she crying? Is it still arousal? I want to speak to her, to reassure her, but I feel like the wind has been knocked out of my body. The knot is still thumping, making coherent thought almost impossible.

Desperate to comfort the female I have just taken as my own, I use the only tool currently at my disposal. I begin to purr.

Almost immediately, her trembling starts to subside. Deliberately taking deep, slow, circular breaths so I can hum for her without interruption, I focus entirely on Emma, marveling at the way I can detect her mood shift in her scent.

Where before, there was a potent cocktail of spicy fear and honeyed arousal, both have abated somewhat. There's still an undercurrent of lust, but something else has overtaken the fear. I'm not entirely sure what it is but she's no longer shaking, so I'm assuming it's a good thing.

The knot is softening, and I'm amazed at the pang I feel in my chest at the thought of pulling out of her. Of no longer being joined to her in the most primal and natural of ways.

Then I remember that, in the throes of my climax, I did something to ensure I'll be joined to her in every and any way I choose, forever.

I gave her the claiming bite.

Once an Alpha has bitten his mate, she belongs to him. He can sense her presence and her absence as surely as he can feel the rain on his skin. He is attuned to her moods, her wants, her pain. And he will not let anyone or anything come between them.

This little Omega might not know it yet, but this first fuck was just the start. She was made for me; her soft, hot little body was created solely for me to own, to possess, to enjoy, to cherish. I will rut her, purr for her, provide for her...

I will breed her...

Emma is mine now.

SEVEN

Emma

I DON'T KNOW what's happening to me. I don't know where I am. I don't know anything, really—except that when Khan begins to make a strange, rumbling noise, it feels like a warm silk blanket being draped over my naked body. Where his growling made wetness gush from my pussy in a way that should be a biological impossibility, this new sound makes me calm and sleepy, like I've been given a strong tranquilizer.

His huge cock is still inside me, my legs are wrapped around his hips, the spot on my neck where he bit me is throbbing painfully. I should be untangling myself, fighting him off, giving him a lecture about consent, and demanding that he take me home. Instead, I'm curled up against his huge, hard chest and feeling inexplicably calm.

What was in that injection those lizard things gave me? I don't recognize myself; it's like I have no control over my body's response to anything.

I've had good sex before, but what we just did... it was on another level entirely. I didn't know anything could feel so wonderful. And even though my pussy is raw and aching, even though I came so hard and for so long that I thought my orgasm would never end, I find myself wanting more.

I breathe him in, absurdly wishing I could stay like this in his arms forever. My thoughts are all over the place and I just let them run through my mind, too exhausted to examine them in much detail.

Something happened to Khan's cock as he was fucking me. It grew bigger in some way—long after it was already hard. Shortly before he came, there was a searing pain at the entrance to my pussy, and it felt like he was no longer able to thrust and withdraw the way he had been doing. Even now, it feels lodged inside me. I wish I had the strength to ask him about it.

Funny how I'm thinking about details like that when I should be focusing on the bigger picture. I just got fucked by an alien who rescued me from a slave auction.

I may or may not be on a spaceship right now, but I'm definitely not on Earth.

Nor am I dreaming, unfortunately. This is all too real.

Other beings injected me with something that turned me into a nympho for this huge, purple beast.

How am I still so fucking calm?

We're moving. Khan is carrying me somewhere, his chest still vibrating with what sounds like a big cat's purr. The next minute, we're sinking onto a soft surface...

A bed.

I'm still wrapped around him but I move my leg so it doesn't get crushed as he positions us on our sides.

God, I'm so tired.

I'm filthy, my thighs and groin are soaked with a mixture of my juices and Khan's cum, and I'm still wearing the tattered remains of my club outfit. I should be looking for a shower, new clothes, and a way to get home.

But all I want to do is sleep.

My eyelids are so heavy, I don't resist when they droop shut. Khan's purring is permeating every fiber of my being, as comforting as a cup of hot chocolate on a cold, snowy evening.

It's no good. With a little sigh, I allow the darkness to overtake me...

THERE'S a brief second when I wake up where I have a fleeting hope that it was all a dream. Then I see Khan looking down at me, his dark eyes glittering with an emotion I can't read.

"Emma," he says softly.

God, his scent... it makes my tummy flutter and my heart pound.

What is wrong with me?

I take a moment to assess. While I'm still dressed in my torn clothing and lying on the bed, he's withdrawn from me and is sitting up, gazing down at me. He's wearing a tunic now instead of that leather harness. It looks like a modern version of something the Romans would have worn, in a shimmering shade of dark blue, and sets off his lilac coloring and midnight hair perfectly. While he smells as wonderful as he did before, the underlying musky note of fresh sweat has gone. He must have showered while I was asleep.

I suddenly want a shower more than I've ever wanted anything in my life—except, maybe, how badly I wanted Khan a short while ago.

Sitting up, I wince at the sudden, sharp pang in my sex. Then my fingers go to my shoulder, where he bit me. I can't see the wound, but I can feel the raised, hot flesh.

He's watching me and, when he sees me fingering the bruise he put on me, he says, "Mine."

"Yeah, you did that," I say ruefully. It's a good thing I'm a masochist. I'm not sure the average vanilla girl would have reacted quite so calmly to being bitten that hard.

I can't read the expression in his eyes, but he seems to be receptive, so I decide to ask for what I want. "I need a shower," I tell him, praying that the translation software will make it clear to him so I don't have to perform any more ridiculous mimes. "Get clean. And new clothes."

He nods. "Of course."

I'm slightly taken aback. That was easier than I thought.

He holds out a huge hand and I take it, letting him tug me off the bed. I follow him on unsteady legs as he leads me to the bathroom and sets about twiddling buttons and levers.

When he undresses me, I let him. I want to wash myself too badly to care about nudity or what he might think of my body. We fucked in such a desperate hurry that we both basically remained clothed, only tugging aside the material that was in the way, so this is the first time he's seeing me naked. Odd, how the things that would normally matter don't seem to matter quite so much right now.

I step into the cubicle and am unable to prevent my gasp of pleasure as numerous jets of water all flick on at once, somehow already set to the perfect temperature, massaging and soaking my tired muscles, sluicing away the sticky residue between my legs.

It's bliss.

"Do you have anything for me to wear when I'm done?" I ask Khan, tipping my head back to wet my hair.

"Yes," he says. "I'll get something."

"And soap?" Glancing around the shower cubicle, I

spotted nothing that even remotely resembled shower gel or shampoo.

"Here." He hands me a little bottle of something, and I squeeze some of it into my palm.

"Thank you."

"I'll get clothing," he says, then disappears while I work the soap into my skin, marveling at how such a small amount could make so much lather. I use it on my hair, too. It smells divine.

The place where Khan bit me stings like the devil when the water hits it but I somehow relish the sensation; there's a slow, excruciating thump between my legs when I recall the combination of pleasure and pain.

How can I want him again already?

If there was any lingering doubt that none of this is actually happening, that ship has now sailed. Too much has happened, and it was all too vivid, for this to possibly be a dream.

Which means I need to come up with some kind of plan to escape and get back home.

My mind is racing even as I try to just relax and enjoy the shower, and so when Khan returns holding a bundle of fabric, I rinse off and step out, asking him to turn off the water. The panel looks like something out of the cockpit in an airplane; there's no way I could work all those knobs and levers.

When Khan hands me the soft, pale blue robe, I hesitate. I need a towel, so I ask him for one.

"Don't need it," he says. "Just put that on."

To my astonishment, the fabric of the robe is more absorbent than any towel I've ever used. The material is cool and comforting on my damp skin, drying it almost instantly.

I don't have a comb so I rake my fingers through my wet

hair as best I can. God only knows what I look like, but from the hungry way Khan is staring at me, it can't be too bad.

Now that he's in close proximity to me again, his smokey chocolate scent is once more tickling my nostrils, and the unmistakable tingling in my clit is back. It's horrible, the way my body reacts to his mere presence, and I remind myself to remember to breathe through my mouth as much as possible.

Something about the way he smells is a definite trigger for my libido.

Wordlessly, he turns and sets off, and I follow him. What else can I do?

We enter another room. It's just as sleek and silver as the others, but it has something else, too. Windows.

I stare and stare with my mouth open.

The view consists of nothing but inky black darkness, dusted with glittering stars as far as the eye can see.

We really are on a ship, out in space.

I'll be damned.

"Emma." Khan's voice is soft, like a gentle growl, and I turn to look up at his rugged, unusual face. "Are you hungry?"

As if in reply, my tummy rumbles. Best timing ever. Weird, how I wasn't even thinking about food before, but now I'm starving. "I am," I admit.

"Come and sit."

I tear my eyes away from my first sight of outer space. There's a glossy table and two stools in one corner of the vast room. There are bowls and tumblers of something on the shiny silver surface, and whatever is in the bowls is steaming.

Suddenly, I'm scared. What do Ulfarri eat? Please don't let it be something gross, like bugs. Or raw meat. I'm a vegetarian.

Khan has sat down on one of the stools, and he's glowering at me now. "Come and sit," he says again, his tone firmer and more forceful than it was before. There's no doubt about it, there's a definite Dom quality about him.

I hate that it turns me on. Even so, my legs are moving toward him before he's even finished his sentence.

Once I've reached the table, I sink down onto my stool, still too afraid to look in the bowl in front of me.

"Eat," he says, lifting a spoon and plunging it into his bowl.

I watch him scoop what looks a lot like porridge into his mouth and swallow it quickly, hardly chewing it first at all.

Not meat then.

Beyond relieved but still filled with trepidation, I pick up my own spoon and try some of the thick gruel.

It's so bizarre. The texture is gross—thick, grainy, and warm—but it tastes of nothing at all. Literally nothing. Like when you have a cold and lose your sense of smell.

After the first spoonful, I have to force myself to take another, but the gnawing pangs in my belly help me along. This food might be weird, but it's doing what it's supposed to do: filling me up.

My hand shakes a little as I pick up the tumbler and take a sip of the clear liquid. This, too, tastes of nothing at all. It seems like water, or some alien equivalent.

Khan devours his portion, emptying his bowl before I've even finished half of mine. Then he sits there, watching me intently, making me feel like I'm under a microscope. He doesn't ask whether I'm enjoying the food. Does he know it would be a dumb question, or is it because he doesn't care whether I like it or not? Or maybe Ulfarri just aren't into conversation at the dinner table.

I wonder what time it is.

I wonder what *day* it is.

I wonder what they'll say at work on Monday morning when I don't show up.

That last thought is like a punch to the gut. I spent *weeks* working on that campaign, getting it ready for Monday's presentation. The client is flying in all the way from San Francisco.

Fuck.

It's not fair. I've worked so hard to get to where I am. I was only promoted to creative director a few months ago. And now I've been abducted by fucking aliens, and everything I've sacrificed so much for will be lost if I don't get home in time.

Provided it's not too late already.

My appetite ruined, I put down my spoon and scowl at Khan. "Where are we?" I ask.

He raises a thick, inky blue eyebrow, then his gaze slides to one of the huge windows in silent remonstration.

"I know we're in *space*," I add. "I'm not a total moron. But where are we going? Where are you taking me?"

Such a cliché line but a valid question, nonetheless.

"Home," he says.

A sudden bubble of hope forms in my chest. "Home? You mean Earth?"

A crinkle of confusion appears on his forehead. "Earth? No. Home. Altrim, Ulfaria."

The bubble of hope bursts with an almost physical pop of disappointment. "What's there?"

"My planet. My kingdom. Your new home." He says these things so matter-of-factly, as if every word wasn't destroying me.

I swallow hard. What's the best way to handle this? Do I appeal to him? Play along? Argue?

The sudden prick of tears in my eyes takes me by

surprise. I don't usually cry. I prefer to suppress my emotions, and bury myself in work.

Blinking furiously to ensure none of the moisture spills over my lower lashes, I take a deep breath, then immediately regret it as the aching pulse between my legs is renewed. How in the capital eff am I meant to have a serious conversation with Khan's scent constantly distracting me?

I wish I did actually have a cold. This would be a lot easier.

"Look," I begin at length. "I'm sure... Ulfaria... is a lovely place, but I don't actually want to go there. I need to go back to Earth. *My* home."

His hooded, glittering eyes narrow for a brief moment, and I try to work out what emotion I just saw flicker across his face. Was it pity? Anger? It definitely wasn't lust. I've seen enough of that over the past few hours that I can recognize it easily. "No," he says. "You're my mate now. I claimed you."

In shock, forgetting I'm on a stool, I lean back and almost go flying, only just regaining my balance in time.

The huge alien male sitting opposite me doesn't miss a thing, and the corner of his mouth lifts when he realizes how close I came to going ass over tit.

Embarrassment makes me angry. "I don't care what you think you did," I say furiously, shoving my still damp hair over my shoulder in an attempt to recover some kind of dignity. "I don't know what's going on, what you think you're doing, what you think you're entitled to just because we... had sex... and you then helped me wash... and fed me wallpaper paste. But I have a home, on Earth. I have an apartment I lovingly decorated, and a job I've given up everything for. Literally *everything*. You don't get to swoop in and snatch all that away from me."

Khan has been listening intently during my rant, his face growing darker and darker. I should probably be treading carefully right about now, but I'm honestly beyond giving a crap.

"I saved you," he says thunderously.

"*Saved* me?" I can't prevent the disbelief in my tone. "You kidnapped me! Then you made me..." I blush, remembering how wanton and desperate for him I was. Even worse is the fact that I still feel that way. If he came over to me now, and I breathed him in...

"The Buruwr had the winning bid. Do you know where you would be now if I hadn't rescued you from him?" Khan says in a low, menacing voice.

"No." *What is a Buruwr, anyhow?*

"Tied to a cold table, naked, beaten, every one of your holes being used with no regard for your safety or wellbeing, let alone pleasure—"

"I don't want to know!" I bleat.

He keeps talking anyway. "On Ulfaria, I'm a king. You will be my queen. You will have anything your heart desires—"

"My heart desires that you take me back to Earth!"

"—and in return, I will breed you; we will have many heirs. You're an Omega, that is your purpose."

"The fuck it is!" I'm on my feet now, shaking. "My purpose is to live on Earth, where I belong, with my family and friends, not to mention the career I worked my butt off for! You don't get to kidnap me and decide what my life is meant to be like!"

He can't know that he's hit a sore spot, but he has. I don't want kids. Never have, never will. The women in my family seem to think that's all females are good for: to be barefoot and pregnant, serving some entity with a penis. I don't share that view, not in the slightest. I might be submissive in the bedroom—and god knows, I struggled enough admitting that to myself—but outside of that, I'm an independent woman, through and through. My art led me to my career, which I excel at, and which has become my purpose in life. And nothing is going to change that, especially not some freakishly large, alien alpha. I don't care how good the sex is.

"You need to take me home, right now!" I continue, but even as I'm speaking, the fight is going out of me. Khan has gotten off his stool and is now approaching me, and his scent...

"Hush, little Emma," he says quietly, "there is no need to fight. Fate has brought us together, and this," he reaches out and traces the mark he put on my neck, "has bonded us forever."

His slightest touch causes a hot, wet gush between my thighs and I clench them together, biting back a whimper of desire. The bite is sore and even so, the way he's caressing it, the way he's looking at me, somehow makes me want to throw myself into his arms.

Desperate to get away from my own need for him, I take a step back, then another.

But Khan pursues me with an unreadable expression on his face—until my back hits the wall with a dull thud.

There's nothing I can do.

There is no escape.

I'm trapped.

EIGHT

Khan

LITTLE EMMA MIGHT BE BACKING AWAY from me, but I can smell her arousal, and don't need to touch her to know that she's already producing a river of slick to ease my path. The look on her face, however, is one of outrage, not desire.

I'm torn. Part of me understands that she's in a strange place, and wants to go home. The other part is driven only by the primal need to rut, and doesn't give an Ulfdamn about her feelings. I've waited and hoped too damn long to find an Omega. I'm the king of Altrim, and more than anything I wish to sire heirs. Without an Omega, that's impossible. But now I've met her, things are different. So if she thinks I'm going to let her escape now that I've finally found her...

"Emma," I say gently, reaching out to stroke her cheek. She's staring up at me with wide eyes. They're such a deep blue, just like the dusk sky at Altrim. I could look at them forever.

In fact, I intend to.

"Don't touch me!" she snaps, ducking her head away from my fingers.

I have to resist the urge to shake her. The Alpha part of me is growing impatient to have her again. I'm rock hard, my cock throbbing. I crave being inside her wet heat more than I've ever wanted anything else. But I know I need to tread carefully. I want her happy, not upset. "Am I not taking care of you?" I ask. "I gave you food, a shower—"

"Yes, and I appreciate that, but I still want to go home. To Earth."

What is there that is so important? Why is she so keen to return? Does she have a mate there? That thought hits me like a punch to the gut, and I can feel my blood pounding in my temples. Images of her with another male—of another lover touching her, kissing her, caressing her—flit through my mind, and my fists clench almost involuntarily. I would kill him. I would tear him limb from limb. Emma is mine. She belongs to me, to nobody else. "Why?" I manage, barely keeping my sudden jealous fury in check.

She looks at me as if I'm stupid. "Why do *you* want to go home?" she retorts at length. "It's my home! My apartment, my friends, my work—"

"Work?"

"Yes!" Her expression is incredulous, and it's irritating me. "You know, what you do to earn money. To make a living."

I'm taken aback. Omega females don't work on Ulfaria. They love, and nest, and take care of those around them. Heal the sick, create art and music, and cherish their mates. And procreate, of course. "No," I tell her. "You don't work on my planet. You don't have to. I will take care of all your needs."

She's looking at me like I've grown another head. "What if I want to work? If I *need* to?"

She's a smart one, I'll give her that. "You won't have time, anyway," I say. "You'll be busy rearing our offspring."

Now, her pretty little face is as dark as a thundercloud. It's adorable, but I'm beginning to tire of this conversation. "The hell I will!" she barks.

Where I come from, females know their place. They treat males with deference and respect. And if they don't, they're made to. Emma is different, and females on Earth seem to be raised to feel as if they're equal to their male counterparts, but she will have to adapt.

Reaching out, I grip her slender, pale throat. Immediately, she stills. Her pulse is fluttering wildly against my fingertips as she gazes up at me. I could snap her neck in a heartbeat, yet even so, there's defiance blazing in her eyes. I have to admire her spirit.

"You will do as you are told," I tell her in a low voice. "Or I will make you."

To my absolute astonishment, her reaction is instantaneous. Her eyes go cloudy, and I catch a much stronger whiff of her arousal. Could it be that she enjoys being threatened?

Surely not.

"You will do as I say, little Emma," I continue, watching her intently to see how she reacts to every word. "Or I will punish you until you do."

Her moan is almost inaudible.

Almost.

I can feel her desire throbbing through our bond.

Sliding my free hand between her thighs, I'm not surprised to find her dripping; her pussy swollen and hot to the touch.

"Does that thought arouse you?" I ask, finding the little nubbin that gives her so much pleasure, and tracing tiny circles around it. Intriguing that the threat of punishment could excite her so much, but if that's what she wants...

"No," she whimpers, closing her eyes, her long lashes fluttering against her flushed skin.

"You're lying," I growl, giving her pleasure button a savage pinch. "Don't ever lie to me, Emma."

She lets out a cry not unlike the ones she gives when she's climaxing, and it goes straight to my groin.

Ulf, I'm hard.

"Please," she whispers. "Please don't..."

"Don't what?" I prompt, when she trails off.

"Don't... do this... to me."

"Do what?" I cup her sodden pussy in my palm and begin to grind, relishing the way her puffy lips are sliding against my skin. "This?"

"Oh, fuck..."

She's leaning up against the wall and my hand around her throat is keeping her steady but even so, I notice the way her knees buckle.

Suddenly, I'm aware of just how much power I have over her. I can make her feel good, I can make her hurt, I can make her scream, or cry, or gasp. It calls to the most elemental part of me—the primal hunter. She's weak. She's prey. I can do whatever I like with her.

I'm no longer thinking clearly. I just react on instinct. Removing my hand from between her legs, I readjust my grip on her throat so I'm holding the back of her neck, spin her around, tug her back a little way, and bend her over. Yanking the hem of her robe up over her buttocks, I raise my arm and bring my palm crashing down on one plump, white ass cheek as hard as I can.

The slap echoes around the room and Emma lets out a strangled cry—but there's hunger in her tone, not pain.

"Or this? You like this?" I snarl.

There's a perfect imprint of my big hand on her pale skin. The edges are raised and scarlet, and it has to have hurt, but all I can smell is her slick. All I can feel is her desire. I slap her again, on the other cheek.

"This is how we discipline females where I come from," I tell her. "They don't enjoy it, though. I get the feeling you're enjoying it..."

"No!" she yelps.

"Don't lie to me!" Suddenly furious with her for being dishonest, for thinking I'm so stupid that I don't know exactly how aroused she is, I push her down further and vent my anger on her naked butt, raining hard slaps down on it as fast as I can, until her ass cheeks are a hot pink, with mottled red showing through where she's already beginning to bruise.

Emma remains utterly still throughout, not trying to wriggle out of my grasp, not begging me to stop—just taking the punishment until I decide she's had enough.

But I don't miss the way her bared cunt now glistens with proof of her lust, or the way she was panting as I slapped her over and over again.

Ignoring the pounding ache of my cock, I once again slide my palm over the rigid little button between her thighs, dragging it back and forth.

Emma lets out a garbled howl and comes hard, her entire sex contracting and spurting slick into my hand.

I don't let up; I continue to crush my rough palm against her fluttering pussy even after she's finished climaxing, until she's finally begging and writhing, trying to get away from the stimulation.

I deliver a hard slap between her legs, then lean forward and smear her slick over her mouth, nose and chin. "This, right here, proves that you enjoy being punished," I growl.

"It proves that you lied to me. Don't ever fucking lie to me again."

I'm controlling her, humiliating her, punishing her... and what she does next is almost my undoing.

Emma opens her mouth, and begins to lap her slick from my fingers.

Snatching my hand away, I free my raging erection and plunge it deep inside her tight, wet heat in one fluid movement, fucking her from behind, gripping her hips to hold her in place as I take what's mine.

It's such a hot sight: Emma bent almost double, limp and unresisting as I pound into her, her scarlet, mottled ass cheeks bouncing against my pelvis as I thrust.

Reaching down, I thread my fingers through her hair and grip it tightly at the roots, close to the base of her skull, tugging her upright until her back is arched and I'm almost lifting her off the floor with the violence of my thrusts.

I've never known anything like it—everything else has ceased to exist. Nothing matters except the way this female is trembling in my arms; the heady scent of her slick; how her tight cunt is stretched wide around my cock as I plunge deep.

I slide my free arm around her, clutching her back to my chest, then push her up against the smooth silver wall, releasing the last leash I had over my self-control as I fuck her with all the savagery my rut demands.

She's letting out ragged gasps, and when I feel her tighten around me, my knot begins to form. "Now," I growl, needing her to climax with me.

My command works. Emma shudders, her cunt snatching at me as she comes, her moans of pleasure turning into a scream as my knot expands, stretching her painfully wide.

My own orgasm barrels through me with astonishing

force, and I can't contain my roar of pleasure as my cock jerks over and over again and I fill the little Omega to the brim with ropes of my thick, hot cum.

Emma was made for this.

Made for me.

NINE

Emma

What the capital eff is wrong with me? As infuriated as I am by Khan, when he's close to me... when I smell his intoxicating scent... when he growls... I'm powerless to resist. I've heard of *the mating instinct* being used as a term in wildlife documentaries but never in a million years thought a human could ever feel anything close to that kind of primal, desperate urge.

And I don't even want to get pregnant.

Getting pregnant would be my worst nightmare.

For all his talk about breeding, is it biologically possible for Khan to knock me up? After all, we are two entirely different species, even if there are several physical similarities.

What the fuck was in that serum the Ogsul injected me with, anyway? Some kind of fertility hormones? No human body should be capable of producing such copious amounts of vaginal lubrication... I've been wet before—I'd even have described myself as soaking, on occasion—but what Khan's proximity induces in my nether region is on another level entirely.

It's like a tsunami of girl goo.

When his knot softens sufficiently for me to be able to extricate myself, I do just that, marveling once more at the rivulets of my juice and his cum trickling down the insides of my legs.

"I want another shower," I tell him, fully expecting him to argue.

Instead, he merely nods. "You remember where it is?" he says.

"I do. You're not coming with me?" To be honest, I'm grateful for the chance to be alone, but I have no idea whether I'll get that shower working on my own.

"I need to make sure we're still on course," he tells me, adjusting his tunic.

Of course... we're on a spaceship, making our way to his planet.

His damn planet. Not Earth. Bastard.

Another wave of fury plows through me but I swallow it down. If he senses my anger, he might do that purring thing again, and that has the same effect on me as a lullaby does on a cranky baby.

Right now, I prefer simple, unadulterated rage. That helps me get shit done.

"Okay," I tell him, tightening the robe around myself. "I guess I'll meet you back in here?"

"Emma," he says, and takes a step towards me. His glittering dark eyes are narrowed, his gaze intent. "Don't think about trying to run away. There's nowhere to go. We're on a little ship out in deep space. You don't want to make me angry, do you?"

I hadn't actually been considering any kind of escape—

and he has a point. "I don't," I assure him. "I just want to freshen up. And as you said, there's nowhere for me to go."

Those words haunt me as I make my way back to the bathroom and stare at the panel of levers and dials. I feel like I need an engineering degree just to get the water to run. After a few failed attempts, I flick one lever up, turn a knob, and water starts shooting out of the main showerhead. I'll take that.

Hanging my robe on a hook, I step into the glass cubicle and proceed to scrub between my legs and the insides of my thighs. My mind is racing at a million miles a minute.

Bright sides first: as alien kidnappers go, Khan isn't so bad. He's quite attractive if you're partial to the huge, muscled, broody type with tattoos, and he gives me multiple orgasms with an ease that should be illegal. As he himself said, I could have it a lot worse. I could be tied down and getting gang raped by any number of the hideous creatures who were bidding on me at the auction.

I could be dead.

I'm not either of those things, which is a good start.

On to the negatives—of which there are several, unfortunately. I'm god only knows how far away from Earth, stuck on a spaceship which is currently heading towards Khan's planet. Where he is, apparently, some kind of king. He wants to make me his queen and have lots of babies with me. If this happens, I will never see my friends or family again. I will never enjoy the career I worked my ass off to get ahead in. I will be nothing more than a glorified broodmare; there to produce heirs and spares. And what if Khan tires of me? What if the males of his species have multiple wives? What if it's freezing cold or boiling hot on their planet? What if all their food and drink consists of that tasteless, gritty gruel and plain water?

Can I live without coffee? Chocolate? Donuts?

The fuck I can!

But he was right when he said there was no escape for me right now. Not while I'm on this ship. If this were the same ship I arrived in, I could go hunting for whatever wormhole spewed me out here—but I'm now one hundred percent certain that when I fell through that mud patch at home, I landed on the spacecraft the auction was being held on, which seemed much bigger, and was filled with all manner of aliens.

Khan must have taken me to this—*his*—ship after I passed out in his arms for the first time.

Joy.

Stepping out of the shower cubicle, I wrap the robe around myself. I didn't bother washing my hair again; there was no need.

The place where he bit me is throbbing again. I keep reaching up to touch it, even though it's sore when I do. It's almost like a compulsion.

In fact, a lot of things have felt that way since I met Khan. I find myself constantly doing things I don't actually want to do. Walk towards him rather than away from him. Feel strangely calm when I have every reason to panic. Let him fuck my brains out even when I want to throttle him...

Once back in the room with the table and chairs—and windows—I begin to pace, clasping my hands behind my back and marching up and down like a belligerent headmaster. Walking sometimes helps me organize my thoughts.

Right, Emma. Plan of action. You're in this situation. What are you gonna do to get out of it?

As of right now, I don't really have many options. I have to play along and let Khan take me to his planet. Ulfarri technology seems to be way more advanced than ours, so maybe there'll be someone there with some way of helping me get back to Earth.

Or, I still might be able to persuade him to change course and take me home before we even reach his planet. Though I have to admit that isn't likely at all.

I sigh, flicking my hair over my shoulder before resuming my pacing. I shouldn't have thought about coffee before. Now I'm absolutely desperate for one. I want a grande latte macchiato, topped with whipped cream and caramel swirls...

I also want something else. Blankets. I want warm, soft blankets, and scented candles, and stuffies. Big, cute, plush animals, like the giant fluffy dolphin I was given as a kid.

Now why would I want any of that stuff?

To make a nest.

I hear that sentence very clearly, as if I said it aloud—in fact, I heard it in my own voice. But I'm certain my lips didn't move. I didn't actually speak.

Am I hearing myself think?

Oh fuck, is this it now? Am I finally losing it?

"Little Emma." Khan has returned, and there's a twist of desire deep in my lower belly as soon as he's just a few feet away.

Will he always have this effect on me? I'm starting to feel like a nympho.

"Khan," I reply, taking a couple steps back, trying to mitigate the way his dark, decadent scent is making my clit tingle.

"Did you enjoy your shower?"

"Well, I got it to work, which is a win as far as I'm concerned," I say.

"Good. Is there anything else you need? We will be landing on Ulfaria soon," Khan tells me.

Great. "How soon?"

He shrugs one massive, bulky shoulder. "Later today."

I let that sink in for a moment. God, I'm so tired. I want to curl up in a soft spot and drift away. How do I ask for what I need without sounding like a five-year-old?

"Bed," I say at length. "I want to go to bed."

Khan's face lights up, and I curse inwardly. "Not to matc," I say. "To rest."

"Rest?"

"Sleep. I'm tired," I admit. It's true. I don't know what time or even what damn day it is, but I feel like I could sleep for at least twenty-four hours straight, given the chance.

"Then let's sleep," he says, and the next moment, I've been hoisted into his massive arms and he's carrying me to the room with the bed in it.

Even though I fight it, my nostrils flare and I breathe him in, relishing the way his musk sets my every nerve ending on fire. My nipples tighten under the robe, and I have to clench my thighs around the relentless throbbing ache between them.

Will I ever stop wanting him?

TEN

Khan

I've never purred for a female before I met Emma. There was no need—growling and purring only works on Omegas, and as I was never in rut before, I never had the biological urge.

I love the way my growl affects her body. The way her pupils dilate and darken her gaze; the breathless way she gasps as the slick rushes to her cunt.

I also adore the way my purr affects her. Regardless of how angry or upset she is, the moment I start to purr, she grows meek and compliant, almost kidlike. Best of all, her beautiful face softens, and she seems truly content.

It's the only time she does.

I watch her sleep, drinking in every curve, every line, every texture and color of her gorgeous body and face. I should really go and make sure we're still on course, that there are no issues with the crew—they haven't seen me since I brought my new mate on board.

But it's so hard to tear myself away.

There are nine main Alpha kings on Ulfaria. I am one

of them. But while the others prefer to remain at home, ruling their respective kingdoms, I choose to explore the vast mysteries of space. Anyone who asks why is told about my sense of adventure, my restlessness, my hunger to acquire new knowledge, technology, and experiences.

What I do not tell them is the real, main reason why I began to traverse the universe as soon as I reached maturity.

I wanted to find my mate.

I am rich, I am respected, I am free to do as I please. There is only one thing lacking in my life, and that happens to be the one thing I have always yearned for: a family.

My parents died when I was young, and I have no siblings. That may be why I feel the lack more than the other kings who have yet to find their Omega queens. Why I am not content to sit in my palace and curse Ulf for making me an Alpha when Omegas are so rare—and the soul bond even rarer still. Why I decided to do something about my lot, and take to the stars to find Omegas for my planet.

But I never dreamed I would find such a perfect Omega. And not just any Omega, but the one who was destined to be my mate.

My fate.

Emma is fast asleep now; her chest rising and falling rhythmically. Her soft, shiny hair is spread out over the pillow. I bend forward to drink in her perfume. Her plump lips are slightly parted. My mouth waters, but I resist the urge to lick them.

Her sweet, feminine scent still invades my every cell, but she needs to rest. She has been through so much in a short space of time.

Even so, I cannot understand why she is so unwilling to

come to Ulfaria with me. Why was she so outraged when I informed her that she is to be my queen?

After all, her body reacts to mine the same way mine does to hers. And nothing in all the galaxies could keep me from her now that I've found her. Not now that I've experienced the bond. The mere thought of being away from her for any amount of time is enough to make my gut twist painfully, and for a sharp ache to pull at my chest.

Surely she feels the same way?

Even though it's been my mission for decades, I never expected to actually find my soul mate. I had hoped the Ogsul serum would work on an attractive female to the point where I went into rut upon scenting her. If an Omega's estrus scent sends me into rut, I am able to impregnate her, regardless of whether we have a soul bond or not. And I had reached the point where I would have contented myself with that: a female I find attractive, with whom I can breed.

But there's something about Emma... what I feel when she's in my arms goes so much deeper than attraction. Deeper even than the rut. I can't explain why or how, but I have no doubt that we are soul bonded. Giving her the claiming bite was purely instinctual, but I couldn't have stopped myself from doing it any more than I could will my blood to stop coursing through my veins. My luck in finding her is beyond my wildest dreams, so if she thinks I will allow her to leave...

Just the idea of it, the mental image of changing the ship's course and taking her back to Earth, to say goodbye to her forever... it's enough to make me want to beat my chest and roar with grief.

I could never do it.

My teeth have made a vivid scarlet circle on her neck,

and while the flesh is swollen and looks painful, my heart thumps in my chest whenever I look at it.

My mark.

On my mate.

Binding her to me.

I stop purring, and immediately grow hard again. The rut truly is as powerful and all-encompassing as the legends tell. An insistent pulse echoes through my groin, and my sac aches with need. I resist the urge to reach out and touch Emma, to cup one plump, pale breast, to roll the pink bud of her nipple between my fingertips until it grows taut and she makes one of those delightful sounds of pleasure I love to wrench from her lips.

How would she react if I pinched her nipples, or bit them? Her reaction to pain is as arousing as it is astonishing. Usually, I have to be extra careful with females when I'm fucking them so as not to hurt them—we Ulfarri are renowned for our size and strength. We're descended from generations of warriors, after all. But with Emma, I can be rough. I can be demanding. I can cede some of my control and give myself over to my base biological instinct. She actually enjoys it.

Closing my eyes, I take a deep breath, clenching my fists to stop myself from reaching for her. She needs rest. And if she stays asleep even when I've stopped purring, I will go and check on the crew. They need to be given instructions for our return to Ulfaria. Preparations must be made. The palace must be readied.

And then there's the matter of the Omega serum. If the Ogsul have a way to make new Omegas using Hoo-mans, then every Alpha on Ulfaria has hope. Every Alpha on Ulfaria... and beyond. The kings of my planet will soon catch wind of my return with an Omega. They will covet her; perhaps try to steal her.

They can try, but they will fail. I will destroy anyone who tries to take what is mine.

Emma whimpers and I glance at her face, but her eyes are still closed. I realize I'm growling, and adjust the sound back to a purr. I will deal with the kings later. First, I must instruct my crew to buy, barter, or steal more serum. And then we must source more Hoo-mans. We need to find out how the serum worked so well on Emma, and how she ended up at an Ogsul auction in the first place.

I haven't asked her that yet. There is so little I know about her. But I intend to find out everything. She will have no secrets from me, as I will have none from her.

I stroke her hair and when she doesn't stir, I force myself to rise despite my extreme reluctance. I will let her rest now, and once we've returned home and taken care of the formalities, we can go to bed and stay there until the estrus and rut have abated.

I can't wait.

Giving her one last glance to make sure she's still asleep, I force my focus away from my throbbing cock, and jab the button to open the door.

A captain has responsibilities, and I need to go and take care of mine. Then, when I return, she will awaken, and we'll likely have time for another fuck before we land. If the last couple of days have taught me anything, it's that good things come to those who wait...

ELEVEN

Emma

THE SCREAM IS RINGING in my ears, yanking me out of the deepest sleep I've ever had. My eyes snap open. My entire body is trembling, the scream is coming from me... and I am in the middle of the longest, hardest climax of my life.

I stop screaming but I'm rigid, my abs clenched, my sex clenching rhythmically as wave after wave of pleasure starts at my clit and rolls through my entire body. I'm vaguely aware of Khan sitting beside me on the bed, looking down at me as I shudder helplessly.

The expression on his face is a combination of pride and hunger, and I can do nothing but gaze up at him as he milks every last throb from my clit with his skilled fingertips.

Once the last pulse has abated, I open my mouth to say something, but my words turn into a gasp as, without preamble, he slides two long, thick fingers up inside me and starts plunging them up and down, roughly stroking my G-spot in a way that makes my toes tingle and my entire core clench with the intensity.

I'm making noises I've never made before as he fingerfucks me with ruthless intent, and the next moment, I feel wetness spattering on my skin... on my chest, my face...

Khan is making me squirt. I'm actually squirting all over myself.

It's humiliating.

It's so good, I might pass out from the pleasure.

I'm trying to think but nothing else exists—just this great beast of an Alpha who is forcing me to heights of ecstasy I've only ever read about in books.

Khan is still looking down at me, the hint of a smile curving his lips. His huge arm is the only part of him that's moving—he's making me come undone with apparently no effort whatsoever.

I hate that he has this effect on me.

I want him with a desperation that frightens me.

"Please," I manage, not knowing what I'm even asking him for. "Please..."

His eyes blazing, he removes his hand from between my legs and holds it above my face, dripping my own juice over my chin and into my mouth.

It's humiliating and carnal, and I find myself parting my lips greedily, letting him splash some onto my tongue as another bolt of lust shoots through my lower belly.

He leans down to kiss me then, and the taste and the scent of him just inflame me more. I kiss him back hungrily, my arousal tangy on my tongue, spreading my thighs further apart as he shifts, his lips still glued to mine, lining himself up to replace his fingers with his cock.

My pussy is so wet that he slides in easily despite his considerable girth, and I gasp into his mouth as he makes me take inch after inch, stretching me wide, filling me in a way I've never felt before I met him.

It's as if our bodies were made to fit each other.

Khan begins to move, slowly, breaking the kiss and lifting himself up until he's braced on his elbows, his biceps bunching as he grinds me into the mattress. He's fucking me hard and deep, and I close my eyes, lost in the sensation.

"No," he growls, "look at me!"

I have no choice but to obey and force myself to open my eyes again, his snarled command enough to once again get me to the edge of climax.

His pelvis puts rhythmic, delicious pressure on my clit, and his cock is grinding back and forth over my swollen G-spot, and I might pass out if I don't come soon but it's still building... building.

Then Khan moves once more, sliding one huge, tattooed forearm across my chest until he's pinning me down, making it impossible for me to even writhe with pleasure.

I can't move, I can't breathe, I can't do anything but lie there and have my brains fucked out by this big, gorgeous beast whose eyes have turned almost black with lust.

He lets out a roar and thrusts hard, and that sends me over the edge, white spots dancing in my vision as I shatter into a million pieces. The searing pain that invariably precedes his climax only serves to prolong mine, and I would scream if there were any air in my lungs.

The hot, wet flood of his cum fills me, the spurts coming in time with his movements. Khan's so large that I feel his cock pulse even though I'm so wet, I'm dripping, and now my pussy is drowning as he fills it to overflowing.

With a ragged, shuddering groan, Khan removes his arm from my chest, then leans down to kiss me again, tracing my mouth with his tongue, gently nipping my lower lip, distracting me from the searing heat between my legs where we're still joined.

Even though I've come three times, even though he's

still inside me, I want him again. My body reacts to him in a way I cannot control, and that scares me.

Because, while it's the best sex I've ever had, I'm worried that it's becoming an addiction—one that will be more difficult to break, the more often I give in to it. And since I fully intend to find a way to get back home, Khan and I will part ways.

It's a damn shame he's ruined me for other men.

Forever.

Khan

As much as I wanted to let my little Emma sleep, once I returned from going to check on my crew, I was unable to stop myself.

It was partly the way she looked: her long, slender, pink limbs pale against my sheets, her golden hair tousled around her face, her slightly parted lips.

It was also the need to possess her once more, especially after what happened in the control room.

Ulf help me—this beautiful Hoo-man is making my life all kinds of complicated.

I should have guessed something was up when I entered the cockpit to see Ebel, my lieutenant, looking half sheepish, half mad.

"Where in Ulf's name have you been, sir?" he asked in a furious whisper. Then, without waiting for a reply, "We have an issue. King Aurus is demanding an audience. Now."

"Why didn't you comms me?" I snapped.

"I did. Several times." His eyes dropped to my bare wrist. *Ulfdammit.* I forgot to put the damn comms unit back on after my shower.

"Fuck. Has he been waiting long?"

"King Aurus doesn't wait for anybody, not even a fellow king," Ebel said. "You know that. He said you were to contact him the moment you received the message."

I sighed and rubbed the back of my neck. This was unusual. Aurus takes only a passing interest in my travels, preferring to wait until after I return to hear if I have anything interesting to report. "Fine," I said, suppressing the irritation in my voice, "get him linked up."

"Right away, sir," Ebel said, moving fluidly to the panel of controls. As he worked to establish a communications link between us and the Golden King, I schooled my face into an expression of boredom. The Nine rule Ulfaria equally, but we keep to our own kingdoms. There was no reason for Aurus to contact me. Had something happened at home? Was Ulfaria being invaded?

"Khan." Aurus's deep voice reverberated around the control room, his chiseled face filling the comms screen. His golden eyes flashed, and his lips were compressed into a tight line. Behind him, lines of Alphas in golden armor stood at attention. A show of strength. Perhaps we *were* being invaded, I thought—but then Aurus would look gleeful and excited, not angry.

"Aurus. To what do I owe the pleasure?" I forced myself to be calm and polite.

"Come now, Khan, you know the answer to that," Aurus said. "We were so excited when we heard the news, we decided to come and see for ourselves."

"Sir," Ebel muttered, and touched a panel to fill a second screen with a jarring image.

Even before I looked, I knew what to expect, and what I saw on the screen only confirmed it. The forest-covered mountains of my homeland. The palace of waterfalls—*my* palace—with the pristine view marred by ship after golden ship. Aurus traveled to Altrim—to *my* kingdom—with his entire fleet. There were golden ships as far as the eye could see, glinting in Ulfaria's three suns, blocking me from entering my own port.

"You've never sent me a welcoming committee before," I said, my voice tight, forcing myself not to clench my fists in case he could see it.

"You've never returned with an actual Omega before," Aurus retorted, his tawny eyes growing dark with an emotion I couldn't identify. Lust? Anger? Irritation? "We've set up a council meeting to see for ourselves. You will bring her to the meeting, and tell us how you came to find an Omega—the first in an age."

For a brief moment, I broke eye contact with him to survey my small crew. Aurus knew about Emma. Someone leaked the information and betrayed me. Ulf help them.

I gave Ebel a slight nod, which he returned. He will seek out the traitor and find out which one of them violated my trust, and told Aurus about Emma. Whoever it is, he will not live to see another dawn.

"The Omega is frightened and exhausted," I said slowly. "We have traveled far. First, I will introduce her to her new home and then—"

"Did you even *intend* to introduce her to me?" Aurus raised a brow.

I ignored the interruption. "As my mate and queen, my Omega will rule Altrim alongside me." I forced my voice to remain calm.

"Your *mate*?" Aurus's eyes flashed. "You have already marked her?"

The possessive growl erupted from my chest. "Emma is mine. My Omega. My mate."

"Is that so?" Aurus cocked his golden head to one side.

Behind him, his warriors shifted slightly, and light flashed off their gaudy armor. "Would you stake your kingdom on it?"

"I'd stake my life." I met the Golden King's eyes, refusing to back down. The Golden Army is the biggest on Ulfaria, but my ships are faster. I can signal Ebel and disappear across the galaxy, far out of reach, and Aurus knows it. And now it's clear: I'd give up everything for Emma. My life. My planet. My entire kingdom.

"No need for that," Aurus murmured. He raised a hand, and his warriors marched out of view. I didn't relax. I had more to barter with. "I've assembled the Nine Kings for a council. You and your Emma," he purred her name, "are invited to attend."

This wasn't an invitation I could decline.

"Very well," I grunted. Aurus blinked. Had he expected me to fight, or flee? I had another plan: barter. "At the council, we can discuss the new source I've found—one that can provide us with many Omegas."

Aurus lost all semblance of arrogance. "Oh?" He leaned forward in his captain's chair. "What is the source? Tell me."

"I will. At the council meeting." My reply must have sounded too smug, because Ebel cleared his throat. Toying with the Golden King isn't wise. His army of Alpha warriors is larger than my entire country. I do not fear death, but if I were gone, there would be nobody to protect Emma.

"Very well," Aurus barked. "We will discuss this at the council meeting. My ships will provide you with escort. And remember," he pointed a finger at me, "bring the Omega with you."

"I want your word that my Omega and I will be unharmed," I snarled back.

"You have my word. Bring her," he commanded.

The screen went dark before I could reply. *Ulfdamn Aurus and his arrogance.* If he didn't have the largest and most lethal army of Alphas on all of Ulfaria, I would make him pay. And if he tried to take my Omega...

The blood roared in my ears. My cock raged with the need to repossess the Omega in question. Just the thought of anyone else's hands on her was enough to send me blind with rage.

My roar echoing through my ship, I had spun on my heel and stalked straight back to my chamber, where I forced myself to hold back long enough to awaken my mate with a climax before allowing myself to plunge into her tight, wet heat...

Yet even now, after my own orgasm, while I'm still buried deep inside her, the need to reclaim and possess her is so great that I cannot help myself; I begin to move again.

The knot is still solidly stretching her and Emma lets out a yelp of pain at the first thrust, but I slide my tongue over her lips, and her cry becomes a gasp of pleasure.

She's so soft, so wet, so warm. And she's all mine.

I thought the rut instinct was strong before, but this is on another level entirely. As though my lust has been replaced by rage. A scarlet haze blurs my vision as a growl erupts from the very heart of me.

"Khan." There's a note of fear in Emma's soft voice but I register it as some faraway, inconsequential thing. All that matters is that I make her mine again—and I will, whether she likes it or not.

Gripping her silky golden hair, I tug her head back and sink my teeth into her neck as I pound her into the firm mattress. My cock feels huge, engorged, and even so, the knot must be softening as I'm somehow able to thrust more freely now, pulling almost all the way out before slamming back inside her.

"Khan..." It's part moan, part gasp, and it makes my chest ache. Her flesh is sweet and tangy on my tongue as I lap at her skin, licking the indentations my teeth have made on her throat.

Rearing up, I lick my way down over her shoulder to her right breast, biting the taut pink nipple until she cries out and writhes, trying to move away even as her cunt clenches around me. This involuntary flutter of submission pushes me over the edge, and I do what I seem unable to avoid ever since I first laid eyes on this stunning creature: I lose control completely.

Livid with Aurus for daring to even mention the possibility of taking her from me, and somehow furious with Emma for making me feel fear for the first time in my life, I allow the rut to take over and act on sheer instinct, no longer giving an Ulfdamn about anything but what my body is demanding; what her scent is driving me to do; what my possessive urge is screaming in my brain.

I don't want to hear her cries; I don't want to look into her huge, expressive eyes. Right now, this is not about breeding or pleasure—not even my own.

The only thing that matters is marking her as mine, and ensuring that any male for miles around is in no doubt that she is owned and off-limits.

Covering her mouth with my own, I squeeze her other breast hard as I pull out of her, then flip her over, yanking her to her knees before pressing my palm into the small of her back, pushing her face into the bed.

Her ass is shaped like the tip of a spear, I think idly as I split her slick pussy once more with my throbbing cock, gripping the plump cheeks as I begin to thrust, deep and hard.

Every time Emma tries to rise up, I push her back down so the pillows muffle her cries. Since I'm past the point of no return, I'm unwilling to hear any potential fear or pain in her soft voice. I couldn't stop fucking her right now if my life depended on it.

Even if she begged me.

Pushing those unpleasant thoughts away, I focus on nothing but the physical sensation— the pleasure radiating from the point where our bodies are joined, and spreading throughout my entire being.

I thrust harder, my climax already threatening to overwhelm me. My growling is deafening in my ears—or maybe it's the blood pounding in my head. Regardless, I zero in on the smooth lines of her back, the way her little waist dips in before flaring back out into that plump spear shape, and the way her scent fills my every pore.

My knot is about to form again. Her muffled cries grow louder, and despite the river of slick trickling down the insides of her thighs, I can feel her begin to pulse around my rigid length.

That is my undoing. Without conscious thought, I yank myself free of her, lift her up, and spin her around, throwing her down onto her back just in time.

My climax is hard enough to make me see stars as my cock jerks over and over and over again, ropes of my cum spurting out to cover her face, her belly, her breasts, her hair.

It's a primal thing. I'm marking her. She will bear my seed and my scent, she will be covered in it, she will wear it like a badge of honor and a talisman to ward off any other hungry males.

When my orgasm finally subsides, I let out a last, ragged growl, then slump beside her, trapping her beneath my arm, my own cum slick against my skin.

My heart and my cock are both pounding in unison, and I feel more exhausted and drained than satisfied.

But there's also a sense of relief.

Nobody will touch her now.

I would kill them if they even tried.

TWELVE

Emma

KHAN IS PURRING. I'm lying there, covered in his cum, sticky with it, and reeling from the way he just took me without any apparent care or concern for my pleasure, and his low purring is making it impossible for me to voice my feelings.

The sex we had before was rough, primal—painful, even—but what he just did was on a whole different level. I don't know where he went while I was asleep, but it's clear something has happened. The anger is radiating off him like a tangible thing, and even when he was inside me, he felt strangely distant, as if he wasn't really there with me.

For the first time since he brought me back to his ship, I felt genuine fear that he would hurt me, and that only increased when he didn't react to my pleas.

And yet... and yet... his magnetism is so strong that I came anyway—hard—the brutal way he was fucking me, the way his big, strong hands gripped me hard enough to leave bruises, his teeth sending bolts of pain through my core, and the callous way he flipped me over and took me roughly from behind, all combining to send me flying over the edge.

I didn't know chemistry like that could exist.

I was still coming when he tore himself out of my spasming pussy, flipped me onto my back, and spurted all over me. It was hot and humiliating at the same time, and the way he did it was almost methodical, as if he was on a mission to cover as much of me as he could. And while I'd already been aware that he produced copious amounts of seed, I hadn't realized quite how much it was until it was splashing on my skin—trickling down my chin, over my breasts, down my ribs, and pooling in my belly.

It felt feral, in a way, like an animal marking its mate.

I want to ask him about it, ask him what's wrong, ask him why he's so angry, but his purring is making me sleepy and calm, unable or unwilling to even speak. I snuggle against his hard, bulging muscles, breathing in his musk, and close my eyes as his arms clamp around me like a protective vise.

Whatever the issue is, we'll sort it out in a minute. I just need to rest for a few moments...

Khan

"Khan?" Emma's lips part as I set her on her feet. She begged me for a shower, but I refused. Instead, I allowed her to wash her face and brush her hair before rutting her once again. She's drenched in my scent. Dressed in a fresh white robe. I toy with a strand of her soft hair. If I had my way, I'd stay and fuck her again before flying to my kingdom—Aurus and the council be damned.

I pick up the cloak I've chosen for her to wear, to shield her body and swathe her in my scent.

"Are we here?" Emma asks. "At your kingdom?"

"A slight detour," I grunt and grasp the back of her neck, massaging lightly. Her big eyes blink at me.

"Is everything all right?" Her voice trembles slightly. She seems attuned to my moods, as I am to hers, as if through an invisible bond. Right now, she feels trepidation tinged with curiosity.

"All will be fine." I bend down to meet her eyes. "I will never allow anyone to hurt you."

"I know." Her trepidation disappears, leaving only curiosity. Her pupils widen, drowning out the blue. Her perfume starts to rise. If I don't hustle us out now, I will not be able to keep from fucking her once more.

And I'd prefer to get this over with.

I tug off the white robe and sweep the cloak around her. It's one of mine, and it swathes her form completely. Perfect.

"Um, Khan?" Emma lifts an arm. Her limbs are swimming in the extra lengths of fabric. A third of the cloak pools at her feet. "I'm not sure I can walk in this."

"No need." I scoop her into my arms. She grasps my shoulders as I carry her out of our rooms, and down the corridor to the exit bay.

My crew has assembled there. They know I've been summoned to the Kings' Council.

When I appear, they snap to attention, standing in two lines on either side of the gangway. Beyond them, the Golden Kingdom glitters.

"You have your orders," I say. Ebel nods, and the rest strike their chests to acknowledge my command. As I pass Ebel, he flicks his eyes to a crewman standing down the line.

He found the spy, and placed him at the end of the formation. Excellent.

As I stride down the gangway, I shift Emma to my left side. The traitor is a younger member of the crew. He wears his hair long, like mine. Perhaps he has delusions of replacing me. My fist curls over the handle of my scimitar.

I pause in front of him. "Was it worth it?" I ask.

The Alpha's eyes widen. "Sir?"

"What did he promise you? Riches? Gold? Or a chance at the Omega?"

The traitor's eyes flick to Emma's face. Big mistake. My blade is out and flashing, separating his head from his neck with a sweep of my arm. I angle sideways to shield Emma from the blood spray.

She gasps. Before the body has even toppled, my scimitar is sheathed—the blade feeds on blood and flesh, and therefore cleans itself—and I'm moving down the gangway, striding towards the gaudy golden palace shimmering in the suns. Ebel calls for a crew member to kick the remains out of the ship. The traitor's body can rot on Aurus's doorstep. It can be a message to him, and all others who might try to come between me and my Omega.

There's a reason we're called the *Brutal Ones*.

Emma

It's bright outside. I duck my head against Khan's shoulder to hide from the glare. He continues walking, and the brightness intensifies, like we're going into the sun. The heat hits my face, simmering, along with a rich, spiced scent. After the cool, recycled air of the ship, it's a shock.

In the distance, I hear a sound like chirping birds, and a breeze stirs the thick heat.

Slowly, my eyes adjust. And I find I can raise my head. But the brightness is still there. It's not the sun. It's this planet. Ulfaria.

The road is made of shining metal in different shades of honey, bronze, and gold so bright, it's almost platinum, depending on how it catches the light. Multiple suns blaze in the pale lavender sky ahead. The ground under our feet shimmers with blinding glare.

"It's so beautiful," I whisper.

"Aurus likes his gold." Khan sounds dismissive.

No wonder the heat is like walking into an oven. I dip my head, grateful for the oversized hood Khan dressed me in. The fabric seems to have cooling properties. It keeps some of the heat at bay.

"I can walk too, you know," I murmur. "If you give me something less bulky to wear."

"No," he responds, and his Dom tone of voice quells any more resistance I might have had. I have no idea where we are. I can only tell that Khan is not happy.

When my eyes adjust further to the glare, I angle to look where we're going, and gasp. The long golden road is actually a bridge, suspended in air. Lining each side is a row of statues, in helmets and suits of golden armor. Towering at the end of the bridge is a shimmering golden palace.

We pass the first row of suits of armor and I realize eyes are glittering through the visors in the helmets. They're not statues—these are soldiers, standing unmoving in the raw heat. There are so many of them.

I shrink against Khan. There's a low growling in his chest, but it feels different to the way he growls when he's horny. It's like he feels threatened by the soldiers. This must be why he's not happy.

"Khan, what's going on?"

"Do not fear. This will not take long. I will not leave your side."

He won't even let me walk. The growl rumbles in his chest as he carries me all the way to the palace, and up the giant, pale gold steps. The columns tower twenty stories over us. Inside, it is cooler, but no less overwhelming. More gold columns line the massive corridor ahead.

The further away we get from the entrance, the less oppressive the heat. Every so often, light streams from the ceiling to create pools in between the giant columns, showcasing large, tree-like plants—if trees had silvery white trunks and large, black or pink leaves. It's a jungle in a palace. In the distance, creatures twitter and call to one another. The sound is welcoming, somehow normal.

I push back my hood, wishing Khan had let me shower. That he hadn't fucked me again right after I washed my face. My hair is a little sticky.

"Be still, Emma," he commands. I drop my hand from my hair with a sigh. What with his seed on my skin and me wearing his cloak, his scent is emanating from every part of me. He did this on purpose.

A sharp click-clack of metal on metal sounds ahead. Several armored soldiers march into view, emerging from between two columns. The warriors are huge—even bigger than Khan, who was the biggest being I've ever seen. If their armor delineates their muscles, they're built like linebackers, and make up the biggest, baddest football team ever. Alpha football. Probably something to see.

"Welcome, Majesty." The lead warrior strikes his fist to his gold-plated chest. Khan growls, and keeps walking. The helmeted heads turn to watch as we pass. The sensation of eyes on me makes my skin crawl.

Only when there's more distance between us and the

warriors can I relax. The deeper into the palace we go, the less light there is. There are no more trees, and the twittering sounds recede. "What is this place?" I whisper.

"The Golden Palace," he responds. "Aurus has called a Council of Kings."

That does not sound fun. "Why?" I ask.

"They wish to behold what I have claimed." His eyes glitter.

"Huh."

"You will behave," he warns, and pats my behind. I flush, remembering how he spanked me back on the ship. His hand was harder and more painful than some paddles I've encountered, and while it turned me on at the time, right now, I'm too sore and tired to want more. A new contingent of hooded figures has appeared to greet us, emerging silently from the shadows. They aren't as massive as the warriors earlier, but the way their deep hoods shroud their faces is still creepy.

"Welcome," the lead figure says as Khan approaches. We've reached the end of the corridor. The light's receded, and the air is still. Ahead are two massive doors made of beaten metal, like brass. That color looks muted after all that shiny gold, but the effect is no less impressive. "Aurus, the High King of Ulfaria, greets you. We congratulate you on this auspicious day."

Khan says nothing. I peek at the hooded figures. The one out front is in a dark purple robe, and his buddies behind him are all in lighter shades of greyish lavender. Their robes are the same style as the one I'm wearing.

"Is this the Omega?" The lead figure gestures to me. "We have prepared a room for her, with bedding and refreshments—"

"No!" Khan's growled response echoes throughout the shadowy corridor.

The robed figure bows slightly.

There's a small pause. Khan's isn't growling anymore, the way he was around the armored warriors. He seems a tad less hostile.

"Take us to your king, magician," he orders. I rub my ear. Has my translator malfunctioned? *Magician?*

The hooded figures bow again, and shuffle to one side.

The grand doors swing outwards with agonizing slowness. Khan waits a minute, then heads inside. The purple robes follow.

The inner room is the size of a ballroom—still cavernous because of the soaring ceiling, but cozier, filled with dim light. Pale glowing orbs seem to float at specific points around the circular room. The floor gleams with an inlay of gold, and what looks like amethyst and other precious stones. The pattern winds up to a large round table made of a shiny black substance, like onyx.

More robed figures stand in the corners, waiting with their hands folded in their sleeves. They've grouped themselves by the colors of their robes: grey, brown, green, and blue.

Khan marches up to the table. The leader of the purple robes scurries ahead to pull out a lilac-cushioned seat. The chair's arms are carved from dark wood. Khan settles into it slowly, but doesn't let go of me, still clutching me in his lap.

I've just gotten somewhat comfortable when the doors across the room are flung open. Out strides a giant with tawny hair, bronze skin, and gleaming white teeth. A golden breastplate covers part of his huge chest. He's wearing what look like brown leather breeches, and carrying a helmet, which he hands to one of the white-robed figures accompanying him. More golden-armored soldiers stream in behind him, taking up guard posts around the room.

"Khan," the newcomer's voice booms. He spreads his hands in welcome.

"Aurus," Khan growls.

"And this is the Omega." There's a hunger in Aurus's voice that makes me want to hide. So I do.

I duck my face against Khan's neck. Immediately, he starts purring. Brave Emma has left the building. Khan hasn't even let me walk, so I might as well play the scared newbie. Which I am.

I'm on an alien planet. I deserve to indulge in a few freakouts now and then.

But I peek out from behind the curtain of Khan's inky hair to study Aurus. He's staring back at me.

"She's so small," he murmurs. "Do you find her adequate to your needs?"

I bristle.

"Quite," Khan retorts.

"And you are to hers?" Aurus merely sounds curious, but Khan growls back before resuming his purring.

Great. They might as well whip out their dicks and measure them against each other. Maybe that's what this council is all about.

"Do we have long to wait?" Khan asks over the loud rumbling in his chest.

"Not at all," Aurus says. "I had hoped you would allow my magicians to examine your Omega—"

"No," Khan barks.

"Very well. Thank you for bringing her."

Khan grunts.

Aurus seats himself and leans back in his chair, signaling to a contingent of grey hoods in the corner. They float forward, each carrying a pitcher or a goblet. Aurus's cup is gold. Khan's is purple. A smaller, lavender-colored goblet is placed next to his, presumably for me.

I'm thirsty, but I don't trust anything Aurus would serve us. Apparently, neither does Khan. He makes no move to drink.

Aurus smirks at us both over the rim of his goblet.

A door clangs open from another side. Apparently, the room has a bunch of different entrances. More warriors in gold armor march in and take their places behind Aurus. A few seconds later, another huge warrior strides in. He's wearing suede breeches like both Khan and Aurus, and a cape of dark green. Another king? A group of figures in robes follows him—also in dark green.

The warrior seats himself without greeting anyone. The second a robed figure places an emerald goblet on the table in front of him; the warrior grabs it and gulps the contents down. Then he takes the whole pitcher, and empties that. I half expect him to belch.

Another door opens, and a large figure enters wearing a grey hood. Behind him is a cluster of silver-robed magicians, followed by a contingent of silver-armored warriors who tower over them. This king keeps his hood on, but the long hair streaming down his chest is the color of ice, and when he seats himself and reaches for his goblet, his hands are pale with black tattoos snaking over the skin.

"Welcome." Aurus raises his goblet to both. "I bid welcome to the Stone King. The Hunter King." He toasts the grey-hooded king and the green-cloaked king in turn. "And to the Wanderer." He toasts Khan.

The Stone King steeples his hands, and leans forward. His face is hidden deep in his hood, but a warning creeps along my spine. He's watching me.

The Hunter King swivels his head in our direction, his movements fluid, with a feline grace. He raises his head, sniffing the air. "Mate," he grunts, and half rises.

Khan's purr instantly changes to a low, warning growl.

"Now, now." Aurus waves his free hand. " Keep to your side of the table. Khan will not like it if we get too close."

Khan definitely doesn't like it. I'm sure each of the kings has his own specific scent, but all I can smell is the leather, chocolate, and smoke essence rising off Khan's skin —and mine. I'm grateful for the oversized cloak sheltering me.

"Can we get started?" This from the Stone King. His voice is soft, with a slight hiss. Majorly creepy.

A gray-robed *magician* brings forth one of the pale orbs by grasping an imaginary string and pulling it forward so the orb floats along in the air behind him. The robed figure draws it up to the table at an empty seat. A bow, and the magician retreats. The orb glows red.

"Welcome, Demon King," Aurus announces.

Another robed figure brings another orb from a different corner of the room. It glows white.

"The King of Ruins," Aurus says. And at last, a third orb—this one glows black. "The Shadow King." Aurus addresses everyone, orbs included. "The Beast King will not be joining us."

I count around the table. There are seats for all of the kings—including the Beast King—plus a ninth.

"Shall we get started?" Aurus asks.

"What of the King of the Wastes?" asks the Stone King, nodding to the empty seat next to his.

"A mere formality." Aurus shrugs. But robed servants are grouped behind each chair, and every seat gets served a goblet, even the empty one, and the ones hosting glowing orbs.

Are the orbs meant to represent the kings? Or are the kings in a far-off land, connecting with the council via the orbs like some freaky alien Zoom?

Aurus rises and leans forward. "I've gathered you here

for the purpose of hearing from Khan. Our Wanderer King. He's claimed an Omega."

"Impossible," hisses the Stone King. "None exist."

"Scent." This from the Hunter King.

"Yes, exactly," Aurus says. "Can't you scent her?"

All the present kings swivel their heads towards me. The Hunter King creaks forward in his seat, like he wants to lunge out of it.

What will happen if these kings rise up to grab me?

Khan is rigid underneath me, as if he's two seconds away from losing his shit. I tuck my face into his chest, locking my hands around his neck and squeezing tight.

"Where?" grunts the Hunter King.

"Where did you find her?" Aurus elaborates.

"A spaceport," Khan answers. "You know how I travel."

"And you claimed her without a vote?" the Stone King asks.

"I am an Alpha King." Khan's voice rings through the room. "I need no permission."

Aurus raises a hand. "Before you start a fight, let our Wanderer King tell us of the serum that creates Omegas."

Khan grumbles under his breath. Aurus is grinning like he's pulled off a magic trick. "Why don't you tell us, Aurus, since you know so much?" Khan says.

"I know barely anything," Aurus says dismissively. "Just that the serum exists. You killed my spy before I could learn more."

Good grief. Aurus is grinning, but the air in the room is getting thicker. The rumble in Khan's chest grows louder. The Hunter King has a dagger out and is flipping it up and down, catching it without even looking. He eyes me curiously but it's the Stone King who's giving me the creepo vibes. I don't want to know what's underneath his hood.

"The serum will allow us to produce more Omegas,"

Khan says. "My men are procuring some now. Making arrangements with the Ogsul, the creatures who invented it."

"My magicians stand ready. They will study the serum so we can reproduce it," Aurus says smoothly.

"But will the serum work on Ulfarri?" the Stone King muses.

"I do not know," Khan says. "The Ogsul and our magicians can attempt it."

"We shall invite emissaries from the Ogsul, and pay them handsomely. They can administer the serum under the supervision of our magicians, and teach the magicians how to synthesize it. I'm sure we all have pleasure slaves we can donate to the process," Aurus says.

I shiver. These poor pleasure slaves are going to be used as guinea pigs in a medical experiment.

"What race is your Omega?" the Shadow King asks. Khan shifts me closer in his arms even though I'm already pressed against him.

"A Hoo-man," Khan offers. "A species from a far-off planet named Earth. The Ogsul were able to procure mine through a portal."

A portal? Sounds like something from a video game, but it's as good a description of the wormhole I got sucked into in the field as any.

"And they can procure more," Khan continues.

"Then if our own Betas cannot take the serum, we can simply use Hoo-man females," Aurus says.

"No," I say automatically, too softly for anyone to hear, but the Hunter King's head snaps towards me again. His eyes are emerald green. He blinks, and I notice his long lashes.

"Yes," Aurus is still talking, "my magicians will discover a way. Khan, my Alpha warriors are at your service if you will provide ships for the emissaries to travel to the Ogsul. Perhaps we can persuade one or two to be long-term guests. My magicians will study both the serum, and the portals."

"Of course," Khan says.

"And if our pleasure slaves do not adapt with the serum, we will use these Hoo-mans instead." Aurus looks at me. "I would prefer one with golden hair, such as this one."

Khan gives a little growl but I'm too distracted. What's happening? They're agreeing to do what? Kidnap more humans? Women like me?

I prod Khan. He doesn't react.

"That settles it," Aurus continues. "The Omega Objective has begun. We shall create the perfect Omegas, using serum, and Hoo-mans if the serum does not work on Betas. We each can choose the characteristics we please."

"I'm not picky," the Stone King hisses. "As long as the womb is an Omega."

Gross. "No," I say, louder this time. "This is wrong. You can't just take women."

"Hush," Khan says. His hand clamps the back of my head, and he presses my face to his shoulder like I'm some cranky baby he's trying to shut up. My mouth is muffled as he says calmly to the others, "My Omega is distressed. You will excuse us."

The others murmur something, and there's a sound of chairs scraping on the floor as they rise out of some kind of sick courtesy. I try to fight, but Khan holds me fast. "Hush, little Omega," he orders. He's walking swiftly to the door. "All will be well."

No, it won't. I want to scream. They're going to capture more human women as pleasure slaves... and then what? Rut them? Claim them as mates? Do what Khan has done to me? I might respond to him, but these other women... I have to save them. I have to do something.

THIRTEEN

Emma

IF THE LONG walk through the Golden Palace to the Council of Kings took forever, the walk back to the ship takes no time at all. Khan keeps his hand on my head, forcing me to cuddle against him. His purr is at full throttle, intensifying with every step. By the time we've left the heat of Aurus's kingdom for the cool air of the ship, my body is responding to the steady, confident sound. The way Khan's chest vibrates doesn't hurt, either. And the smokey chocolate scent rising off his skin makes my mouth water, and my core clench. It makes no sense, but arousal rolls over me, drowning out all logic, pulling me under.

My juices are sliding down between my buttocks as Khan races us to his quarters. He calls orders to his crewmen, but I'm too busy taking deep whiffs of his scent. My tongue flicks out to lick his neck.

A door hisses shut behind us with a sound like the Stone King's voice. It startles me out of my fog. *Human females, portals, serum.* They're going to steal women like me, and turn them into Omegas. *I have to stop it.*

"The humans and the serum—you can't do this..." I pull back to state my case. Mistake. My eyes meet Khan's, and a tsunami of arousal crashes over me. My own scent rises, thick and sweet.

"Omega," Khan purrs.

"Khan, please—"

But he's already pressed me back onto the bed. He lets out a soft, sexy growl and my body shudders, fluid gushing from my sex as my clit throbs. I'm reaching for him, whimpering.

"Hush, little Emma. All will be well," he murmurs. His gentle words bely his violent manner as he rips the robe off me, and swings himself over my body to fuck me.

My protest rises and breaks against the wall of my need, becoming nothing.

Khan

I rut my sweet Omega until her whimpering cries give way to screams of pleasure. Then I rut her some more. The blankets are drenched with her slick and my seed when I finally rise, purring to soothe her. Her little forehead is scrunched, the black pools of her pupils shrinking within the widening band of beautiful, worried blue.

My thumb works to smooth the wrinkles on her brow. Her lips tremble, and I purr louder. Would that I could fuck her into oblivion, but if she is to be my queen, my mate, the mother of my heirs, then I must allow her time to process. Even if I wish to fuck her again right away.

"You have questions," I murmur, tucking her against my chest so my purr vibrates through her. "Ask."

"Who were those kings?" Her voice is low, husky. I

reach for a glass of water on a side shelf and press it to her lips. I must make sure she eats and drinks well when I'm not taking her.

"The planet is carved into kingdoms," I tell her as she gulps down water. "Each king rules there unopposed. Each king is named for his attributes, or the attributes of his kingdom."

She finishes her water and wipes a hand across her mouth.

"More?" I ask, and she shakes her head, so I take her glass and set it aside. I press her head to my chest once more, and comb my fingers through her silky blonde hair, snagging a sticky patch where my seed has dried. A burst of possessive pride warms my chest. "Aurus is the Golden King, so called because his kingdom mines the most gold. They flaunt their wealth with the palace, the golden bridge, and the armor for their army. The Hunter King's lands are mostly forest. He spends most of his days hunting the deadly beasts that roam and breed in the darker corners of his kingdom. I am surprised he emerged. He must have been curious to see an Omega." My fingers encounter another sticky clump of Emma's hair—the result of our messy lovemaking. The scent of our combined fluids is delicious.

I grin against her head. Of all the kings on Ulfaria, I am the one who proved worthy of an Omega. "Then there's the Stone King—"

Emma shivers. "He's creepy."

I swallow a growl. "It was not my wish to expose you to the council. But it was necessary. Aurus would not have rested until he had a chance to meet a real Omega. And his army is the biggest on our planet—of all the kings, he is the most worthy challenge. A victory over him would come at too high a cost. I would go to war for you, Emma, but attending the council was a wiser compromise. Better to satisfy Aurus's curiosity than risk him attempting to kidnap you."

Emma whimpers.

"Do not fear, little Omega. Now, they will know you are mine." I tip her head back to meet her eyes. "The only king you have to worry about is me."

"What about the Golden King? Aurus."

"Aurus thinks of himself as High King. He fought from a young age to win his position, chief among all Alphas in the kingdom of Aurum. But he will not touch you. I will make sure to give him the first Omega."

Her scent flares, the sweet floral notes turning bitter, charred with distress. "Khan... you can't. You can't take human women, and give them to these kings."

"I have no choice. Omegas have disappeared from my species. Only rarely are Alphas born of Beta pairings, and almost never Omegas. We need Omegas. If the serum does not work on Beta Ulfarri, Hoo-man women are our only hope." I tug on her hair and scratch her scalp to soothe her. "We need *you*." I stifle her protests with a kiss, and roll her onto her back to rut her again.

Emma

If Khan was possessive before, it was nothing like now. Time no longer has meaning—he fucks me until I fall asleep. I wake to him bathing me and pressing me to eat and drink, and as soon as I've eaten, he fucks me again. My only reprieve is during the dark, dreamless moments halfway to sleep. Half-answered questions gnaw at me.

What if Khan is wrong, and one of the kings does try to

kidnap me? Aurus, or the Hunter or the Stone King? Or one of the others—the ones represented by glowing orbs? I didn't see them but I didn't really want to. What does a Demon King even look like?

And if the serum doesn't work on Ulfarri, they're planning on taking human females from Earth to make them into Omega mates. Human women—like my sisters, cousins, friends—condemned to a lifetime here on Ulfaria, reduced to no more than breeding machines. Like me. What if the Beta experiment fails—I hate myself for hoping that it won't—and they succeed in getting humans?

I have to stop it from happening somehow. But how? I know nothing of this planet. Of the magicians or the serum or the portals. My only ally is Khan, and he's more interested in fucking me. He never leaves my side—not to eat, sleep, or bathe. We do everything together. He takes me with him everywhere. His purr scrambles my thoughts.

He didn't let my feet touch the ground once throughout the entire council meeting and even now, as we're heading to his own kingdom, he's constantly touching me, either with a possessive hand on my arm, or carrying me as if I were a small child. It's infuriating—I'm an adult, and able to walk by myself. For all his denial, he seems worried some other Alpha will infiltrate the ship, and snatch me away when he's not looking.

That thought is my personal worst nightmare. Khan may be huge and terrifying and gruff, but at least he's familiar now. He also shows glimpses of a caring, tender side, which is reassuring. He won't hurt me. Sure, the way he fucks me is brutal, animalistic, and violent, but I always preferred rough sex anyway. My gigantic masochistic streak is what got me interested in BDSM in the first place.

Which might also explain why I get so damn wet when he manhandles me.

Whatever effect these weird serum hormones are having on me, Khan seems to be feeling the same kind of way. Even though I'm still covered in his cum from the last time we fucked, his gigantic erection digs into the small of my back as we spoon. My pussy aches from the ferocity of our sex, but also with need. We fucked during basically the entire journey from Aurus's kingdom, but my clit is taut and throbbing, and I crave Khan again. It's only a matter of time before his scent turns decadent and chocolatey, and I can't stop myself from rolling over and licking his neck.

I'm addicted to the way he tastes. Smells. Feels. Sounds.

"Here," Khan rumbles. I'm half awake, and he's rolling me into a blanket. He lifts me and I surrender. Khan carries me everywhere—to the bathroom, to the king's council, then back to his ship where he fucks me endlessly. This is my life now.

We leave the cool of the ship, and a sweet humidity hits my face. A breeze is blowing, ruffling my hair.

"Emma. Look."

Opening my eyes, still sleepy from the rocking motion and warmth of the blanket I've been cocooned in, I lift my head and look around.

"This is Altrim," Khan says gruffly, the note of pride unmistakable in his voice. "My kingdom."

We're suspended on a grey platform, hovering over the most amazing scenery I've ever seen in my life—postcards of the most beautiful places on Earth included. A green expanse of thick forest sprawls between a coastline and a mountain range. Rolling hills and valleys slope to mountains bigger than the Rockies, with white caps that rise above the clouds. There are shining expanses of lakes and streams everywhere, all an amazing turquoise blue.

We're zooming over a massive lake, the airship's shadow

reflected in the still water. There are dark clusters down by the lake's edge—dwellings of some sort, I'm guessing. The platform glides up, heading towards a forest-blanketed mountain. Giant waterfalls gush from rocky cliffs, but as we get closer, I realize they're not cliffs. They're carved platforms jutting out from the mountain—some made of rock to blend in with the natural granite, some of glass to reflect the sky.

"My palace." Khan points to the mountain. There are more rocky platforms jutting out from the cliffside at gravity-defying angles. The palace is built right into the mountain, layers and levels of polished rock and glass alternating with thick outcroppings of trees and gorgeous waterfalls. Frank Lloyd Wright-style architecture with an alien spin. There are several waterfalls created by the different layers of platforms. Water cascades over the edge of the highest platform and crashes onto a second platform below, then to a third, a fourth, a fifth—until the side of the mountain is covered with waterfalls. There's a sweet tang in the air. A cool mist rises from the falls.

"It's breathtaking," I murmur. The suns are setting, leaving pale lilac streaks in the sky. The low light turns the surface of the water luminous.

"My home. Your home now, too," Khan says, squeezing me tighter.

Shit. I bite my lip, unwilling to start an argument right now even as a pang of fear clutches my heart. What if I never actually get to go home?

I've emigrated before, from England to the States. But there's a difference between the cultural shock of going from one small English speaking country to a bigger one, versus going from an Earth home to an alien one. No matter how beautiful this planet is. The sky is purple, for fuck's sake. A really pretty purple, but still.

The closer we get to the mountain palace, the more pride emanates from Khan. It's like there's some invisible bond between us, and I can almost sense what he feels. But alongside his glowing feelings of triumph, my feelings of trepidation and worry are growing.

I clutch Khan as we zoom up to the mountain face. An invisible driver docks our ship at the edge of the platform, hovering right over the endless waterfalls. Khan still hasn't put me down but for once, I'm not resenting how he takes charge. I'm relieved.

All this is way too much for me to deal with on my own. I'm too busy trying to comprehend the enormity of everything that's happened and I'm so exhausted that right now, even walking feels like a chore.

If Khan wants to carry me, I'll let him.

For now.

FOURTEEN

Khan

EMMA IS quiet in my arms as I carry her into my palace. My ship docked briefly to drop us off on the platform that leads to my chambers. My crew will not linger here—they will head back to the main port, and then space, to collect Ogsul for the Omega Objective.

I have more important things to tend to. My Omega needs to be soothed, and introduced to her new home.

My footsteps echo as I stride past the flowing water in its own channel. The crash of the waterfall is up ahead. I carry Emma through the light mist and into the cool darkness that is her new home.

A contingent of servants is waiting to greet us. A mix of Betas, and Alpha warriors. Emma doesn't notice. I dismiss all of them but Calla with a sharp shake of my head. Normally, the presence of Alphas wouldn't bother me.

That was before the rut hit me.

Now, with Emma in my arms, it's all I can do not to bare my teeth and snarl at every male who comes within a hundred feet of us. The Kings' Council meeting was its own kind of hell—trying to stay calm enough to have a vital conversation with Aurus the Golden Asshat while holding the most precious thing in the world to me, whose scent drives me out of my mind with lust, and whose fragile little body makes me want to hold her snuggled up against my chest forever.

Unless I'm fucking her, of course.

Emma's eyes are wide and blue as mountain pools. I pause to pivot slowly and let her see everything.

"Do you like it?" I purr.

"It's very grand. But... different. Not like Aurus's palace."

"No, nothing like that." Jealousy roars in my chest. I fight to keep my purr from turning into a growl. "Is that what you prefer? Gold and gaudiness? An excessive display of wealth?" I hate it, but if Emma likes it, I'd be willing to build a replica for her—twice as big as Aurus's, of course.

Emma's face falls. I try to mute my displeasure—it seems she can feel my feelings through our bond. "No. I didn't like it at all."

Her feelings are a riot between us. Confusion, trepidation, overwhelm. My poor Omega is trying to adjust.

A few feet away, Calla waits with her hands folded. Patient and silent. I wish to introduce her but first, I want Emma to feel at home.

"If you have any questions, you may ask."

She bites her lip and points to a glow lamp in the corner. "Are those orbs like the ones at the Kings' Council?" She's curious about the difference between the glow lamps and the comms spheres.

"Not quite." I shift her in my arms so she can study the orb, suspended in the air. "These are merely lights. The ones at the Kings' Council were communication devices that linked with the distant kings. Not everyone is as comfortable on a ship as I am. Most prefer to stay within their own kingdoms. They don't trust Aurus. Which is wise," I mutter the last part.

"It's like magic." Her hand lifts to the orb, then falters. She rubs her head instead, her distress throbbing in the bond.

I grasp her chin, my purr growing louder. I stare into her wide eyes, pouring soothing feelings into the bond. She blinks, her pupils growing, darkness swallowing the blue of her irises.

Soon she will be done with all thought, but she is fighting it.

"Is that why you call them magicians?" she mumbles, her brow still wrinkled. Ulf, she's adorable. "They do magic?"

"Magic tech, yes."

"Magic and tech aren't really the same thing back on Earth..." She sighs. "I have so many questions."

"And I will answer them all," I promise. "But first, let's get you settled." I turn to Calla, now even more impatient to get my Omega into her new nest, so I can rut her in it.

Emma

Khan's palace is like nothing I've ever seen. It's built into the side of a freaking mountain, for one. And there are streams flowing down the platforms and over the edge, creating all those waterfalls. The rush and roar of the water echoes in the huge room we're in now. The towering walls are a mix of smooth and rough stone. For all its grandeur, the room feels like an enormous cave, carved out of the mountain.

Glowing orbs lend a little light but my eyes are still adjusting to the gloom. At first, I didn't even notice the pretty, green-skinned woman in a dark brown robe standing nearby. How long has she been there?

"My king." She gives a slight bow. "Welcome home. We have done as you instructed. Quarters have been prepared."

As overwhelmed and anxious as I am, I don't miss the way her gaze slides over me—cool, assessing. It feels almost judgmental. What did Khan tell her about me? What were the instructions, exactly? *I will be bringing an unwilling female back with me. Build her a pretty prison.*

Refusing to be cowed, I meet the woman's slightly slanting, emerald eyes. She's tall—at least six feet—and is the first female Ulfarri I've seen up close. I bite my lip, and stare. Her skin is the pale green of a ripe avocado, and her hair the dark, rich tint of pine needles. The Ulfarri come in so many shades and colors, my own pale skin must look weird to them.

"Calla." Khan's voice is full of pride. "Allow me to introduce you to my queen. Emma."

I close my eyes, my face heating at the thought of meeting someone new in my current state: naked, wrapped in nothing but a blanket, tousled and smudged from an excess of sex, and covered in dried cum. "Nice to meet you," I say with as much dignity as I can muster, cradled as I am in Khan's huge arms.

"And you, majesta," Calla says, giving another slight bow. Then, addressing Khan once more, "Shall I take you to her new quarters?"

"Please. And have someone bring refreshments."

Calla walks with unearthly grace, the hem of her robe gliding over the floor as if she were wearing rollerblades underneath it. Unable to cope with anything else for the moment, I bury my face in Khan's broad chest, silently willing him to start purring for me. I could ask him but my pride won't let me. What am I, a child needing a lullaby to be soothed?

Instead I inhale his intoxicating, coffee-tinted scent and close my eyes, concentrating on the gentle, rhythmic rocking motion as he carries me.

It's weird how I've gotten used to the way just his smell makes my core leak and throb. Too tired to fight it, I lie limp and accepting, rubbing a silky lock of his hair between my fingers.

At length, we stop moving and I hear Khan say, "Very good. A good start, at least. You will bring Emma anything else she requires the moment she asks for it. Instruct the others to do the same."

"Of course, my king," Calla murmurs. Her voice is low, with a hint of reverence. She must be one of the Betas I heard mentioned at the council meeting. It's nice to know not everyone around here is an overbearing Alpha.

Lifting my head, I look around, but it's pitch dark and it takes a moment for my eyes to adjust. The room is huge, with high ceilings, but any windows it might have are covered by flowing, thick drapes. In the dim glow of a few glittering orb-lamps, I can make out an enormous bed, as well as a table and chairs in one corner, and something resembling a loveseat in another. There is hardly any furniture, but what there is looks sumptuous and comfortable. Suddenly I'm desperate to get clean, and then sleep.

"Would you like me to set you down, little one?" Khan asks.

"Please." Once I'm on my feet, I clutch the cloak more tightly around myself. "Do you think I could have something to wear?"

He shakes his head. "Not yet. After."

"After what?" I'm hoping he's going to suggest a bath but then I hear the change in his tone as he tells Calla to leave, and my heart sinks even as my clit gives a long, breath-stealing thump.

"And ensure we are not interrupted," he calls after the servant, who turns around, gives a quick nod, then vanishes through a door I hadn't even noticed before, seeing as it was hidden behind a drape.

Not a moment later, Khan has pulled me into his arms once again, and his tongue is tangling with mine.

As tired, dirty, and overwhelmed as I am, I'm already coming by the time his palm slides between my bare thighs...

Khan

We followed Calla to the quarters I figured would be best for Emma to make her nest in, as soon as she feels the instinct to do so. Calla's instructions were to make it sumptuous but sparse. I want Emma to be free to choose all the smaller details—colors, fabrics, artwork—herself when the time comes for her to nest.

It's surprising how impatient I am for her to reach that stage. I want her to feel comfortable enough here in my—*our*—palace that she starts making a home not just for herself, but for our offspring.

And the sooner my seed takes hold, the sooner that will happen.

By the time I've dismissed Calla, my cock is raging yet again, throbbing with the need to be inside her. I've rutted Emma so much that I'm sore—so that even though she produces veritable rivers of slick to ease my passage, the friction of her tight cunt walls gripping my shaft now brings an additional element of discomfort.

It doesn't stop me.

Nothing will stop me.

The pleasure still outweighs the raw, tingling ache on the skin of my cock when I thrust deep inside her.

So the minute Calla leaves, I've tugged my little Omega back against me, tilted her sweet face back, and thrust my tongue deep into her mouth. She kisses me back hungrily, mewling, and the scent of her arousal is so thick that I can actually taste it.

I've discovered Emma loves to kiss so much that it's often enough to bring her to the brink, and sure enough, as soon as I slide my hand between her thighs to find her hard little nubbin and stroke it gently, she lets out a great, shuddering gasp, goes rigid, and gushes into my palm.

Drinking down her moans, I keep rubbing, coaxing more slick from her core, suddenly desperate to keep her climaxing. To see how long I can draw out her orgasm for.

Her whole body is trembling but I give her no quarter, drawing tiny, slow, rhythmic circles around her jumping clit, moving my lips over hers in unison with my fingertip, holding her up with my other arm as she comes and comes, her delicious, sopping pussy contracting over and over again.

At length, her gasps of pleasure become pleas for me to stop. Her incoherent mumbling doesn't stop me from kissing her. I know what she's saying even if she's not sure herself. She's begging me to stop stroking her. Begging me to finish wringing this orgasm from her spasming cunt.

I feel powerful, untouchable, proud. I don't know whether it's common for Alphas to feel this way when pleasuring their Omegas or whether it's just me, but something in the way Emma behaves when I'm touching her fuels my dominance, and makes me feel like I could move mountains and conquer anything. It's heady and exhilarating, and making her body bend to my will is better than slaying hundreds in combat, or exploring new planets.

I'm addicted.

She's grinding her hips now, trying to escape my inexorably stroking fingertip, but I splay my other hand against her round, plump ass, effectively holding her in place.

Emma will not escape what I'm doing to her.

I'm drowning in the taste, feel, and scent of her. She's so wet that I can hear it—the unmistakable slocking noise of my fingers slipping over her sex.

It's incredible, but she's still coming. I've never known a female so easy to pleasure or so greedy for it, and wonder idly whether the Ogsul serum has anything to do with it.

If so, the other Alpha kings will be in for a treat.

Still, they must wait their turn. Wait to see whether the serum will work on Ulfarri Beta females, or whether we need to import more Hoo-mans from Earth.

I, on the other hand, do not have to wait.

My cock is as rigid as Emma's little clit, and throbbing so hard, it hurts. Somehow, her pleasure is distinctly linked to mine—as our other emotions seem to be—and her endless climax has my balls tightening and waves of pleasure radiating through my groin, spreading up through my entire body.

Without even touching myself, I'm close.

Emma cries out when I lift her easily and impale her on my length in a single, fluid move—whether it's from relief or pleasure, I don't know.

The steady, rhythmic clutching of her tight heat around my cock is almost enough to send me over the edge and I bounce her on my shaft—once, twice, three times in firm, full-length thrusts before the knot forms and I come with a roar, tugging her down on myself as I grind up into her.

She's engulfed in my arms, pinned in place as I feel my cock jerk within her slick cunt, spurting thick, hot seed deep inside her with every pleasure-filled pulse. Despite the knot, I can feel my cum oozing out of her, sliding down over my balls and thighs, dripping onto the floor, and even so, I'm still shooting into her, the force of my climax making my knees tremble.

Burying my face in her silky golden hair, I inhale her hot honey scent mingled with the unmistakable aromas of our combined arousal, marveling at how tiny and fragile she feels wrapped in my arms, and how vigorously I can rut her despite that.

I would kill for her.

I would die for her.

One thing is clear: I have never felt this way about anyone before. And I thank Ulf for bringing Emma into my life.

FIFTEEN

Emma

The last few days have been a blur. Ever since I arrived at Altrim, Khan's kingdom, I've felt like a prisoner—albeit a pampered and cherished one. My life seems to consist of nothing but eating, sleeping, and being fucked every which way to Sunday. So it's hardly surprising, really, that I'm restless, sore, and unmotivated.

I guess Khan is trying to take care of me in his own, gruff way, but I still resent how he does it. I was relieved to discover that the food here on Ulfaria is different to what I was given to eat on the spaceship, but the taste, smell and texture of everything I've tried so far has been weird, so I'm not eating as much as I probably should, especially when you consider how many calories having sex burns.

And orgasms.

There's not a part of my body which doesn't hurt. And yet, even though my pussy is raw and my clit aches from the slightest touch, I still find myself wanting Khan. Submitting to him when he reaches for me. Coming hard and uncontrollably from his fingers, mouth, and cock. And surrendering to the overwhelming sense of peace which overcomes me when he purrs.

It must be down to the serum, but it's like an addiction. I want him even though I know I shouldn't.

On the second or third day after my arrival at his palace, I girded my ravaged loins and went to explore my new home. That's when I first noticed the extraordinary artwork adorning the walls.

From what I've seen so far, some of Ulfaria's tech is way more advanced than ours back on Earth, while some of it still seems kind of primitive by comparison—but the paintings are unlike anything I ever imagined in my wildest dreams.

They move.

The pictures literally *move*. Waterfalls cascade. Lakes ripple. Clouds drift. Flowers bloom. I don't know whether portraits of actual people would do the same thing, as I haven't spotted any so far, but I plan to find out. And today is the day I'll be able to do that.

I've loved drawing ever since I was little. In a way, that passion and creativity was what got me into advertising. Unable to make a solid living from painting alone, and desperate for a steady career, I decided to pursue design and photography. After I got my art degree, I started at a fairly small ad agency in London, and worked my way up until I had built up a decent portfolio. Then I decided to relocate and move across the pond.

When the agency in Richmond hired me, it was a dream come true. Not only would I get a work visa for the States, but I would be able to move far away from my family in the process. Two birds with one stone. There's way more to graphic design than splattering paint on a canvas, but it turned out I had a knack for it, the money was good, and I got on well with my colleagues—especially Susan who, as it turned out, is also kinky.

There's a pang in my gut when I think about my life back home, so I rake my fingers through my still damp hair, straighten my shoulders, and push those thoughts away. After I raved about the living pictures, Khan offered to invite an artist over to show me how to make them. She's coming today. And even if I wasn't desperate for something else to happen to break up the monotony of my current existence, I'd be super excited about this.

Rippling lakes? Glittering stars? I got so close to the paintings that I bumped my nose, and I still couldn't figure out how they were moving—or even what material had been used to create them. It definitely isn't watercolor, acrylic, oil, or any other commonly used medium I've ever heard of.

Now I'm pacing in what Khan calls the greeting hall, glancing alternately at the giant entrance, and the incredible picture of a river cascading down the side of a mountain.

"Majesta?" One of the Beta servants calls to me from across the room. "Your guest has arrived."

"Please show her in."

I don't think I'll ever get used to having servants. I vaguely remember there being soldiers standing around when we first arrived, but since that first day, I haven't seen a single male—servant or soldier, Beta or Alpha. Khan is insanely possessive. I don't know whether he doesn't trust me around other guys, or whether he doesn't trust them around me, but the end result is the same: I'm surrounded by female Ulfarri Beta servants.

This one, Lilla, is young and pretty, with pastel pink skin and mauve hair. She ushers in the one I assume must be the artist—another female, of course—who is wearing the same kind of robe all the Betas wear. I quickly learned that the robes have different colors depending on the roles the Betas have in society.

The artist's is a deep, sunset orange.

"Majesta," Lilla continues, "this is Deva."

Deva is lugging a big bag, which she sets down beside her. She looks to be roughly middle-aged, with large, dark brown eyes, bronze skin, and russet hair. The markings on her hands and face are like swirls of caramel. "Majesta," she says.

"Emma," I say. "Please."

"Emma." Deva glances at Lilla nervously, like she's wary of addressing me informally. If I had my way, they'd all call me by my name but Khan won't have it. He says I am his queen and I need to be treated as such. My wishes, apparently, don't matter in that regard.

"Would you like some refreshment?" I offer.

Deva shakes her head.

"Thank you, Lilla. You may go."

There's an awkward pause while the servant leaves. All the Beta females glide more than they walk–they have an inherent grace. I wonder whether they're born with it or whether they're taught it somewhere.

"Welcome, Deva. It's lovely to meet you." I'm about to stick out my hand and then remember they do things differently here. No handshakes on Ulfaria.

"It's an honor to be invited. I hear you're interested in learning about art?"

"I am! I specifically want to know how to make these kinds of pictures." I gesture to the one of the river. It's huge, taking up a third of the wall.

A little crease forms between Deva's eyebrows. "You want to create these yourself?"

"I do."

There's a pause. "There is a certain... skill involved. It

takes many years of practice. Not everyone is born with the ability."

Hmm. I wonder whether she's trying to tell me that not everyone has artistic talent, or not everyone is able to use whatever medium makes the pictures move. I know I have the former... "What kind of paint do you use?"

She hesitates as if wondering whether to say something, then bends and rummages in her big bag. Taking out a pot, she hands it to me.

I bring it close to my face and examine it. It's a jar holding a substance which is bright teal in color. The lid on it seems tight. When I tilt the jar, the contents move slowly, so it is liquid, but it's thick. It shimmers in the light. "And how do you apply it?"

More rummaging, then she hands me a tool which looks like a cross between a brush and a feather. The handle is long and tapered, like a regular paintbrush, but up close, the bristles look more like tiny feathers. They're so soft against my fingertip that I wonder how I'll know if I'm using the right amount of pressure.

I may be about to learn how to paint all over again.

"This," I hold up the jar, "is what makes the picture move?"

"No." Deva shakes her head. "Magic dust is what does that."

"Do you have some here?"

She bends back down to her bag and produces another jar. I don't know what I was expecting but the powder in this jar looks like very finely ground flour. No magic sparkles, or even a light shimmer. It seems disappointingly ordinary. "This is what makes the picture move?" I ask again to confirm.

"Yes. But only those with the gift can make that happen."

"The gift?"

She nods. "As I said, it takes many years to learn."

Again I wonder whether she means the painting, or the movement. I guess I'll just have to wait and see. "Do you think you can teach me?"

"I can try." Picking up her bag, she glides over to the huge table I had cleared especially, and starts to lay things out. I recognize palettes, more brushes of different sizes—but all with the weird feather tips—and several jars containing paints in the most exquisite colors. Deva then lays out two sheets of canvas, one at each end of the table. "Majesta—"

"Emma," I correct her automatically.

"Emma. I cannot promise anything. His Majesty will be most displeased if I—"

"Please don't worry about Khan," I interrupt her again. "All I ask is that you show me. Anything I produce—or I'm not able to do—is out of your hands. You won't be held responsible."

The relaxation of her shoulders is visible. "Thank you, Maj—Emma."

As I go to stand in front of one of the canvases, the off-white expanse calls to me, as do the rich colors of the paint jars. The entire scenario ignites something deep in my belly. Excitement. Hope. Potential. I glance over at the painting on the wall, the way the river shimmers as it slithers down the mountain, and it hits me how much I've missed this. As much as I enjoyed working in advertising, nothing I did there ever gave me the same rush as standing in front of a blank canvas, knowing I was about to create. To make art.

I pick up one of the brushes and finger the tip carefully, trying to get a feel for it. Deva, meanwhile, has gone to stand in front of the other canvas. I watch her as she gets set up, and copy her movements as she prepares an array of brushes, paints, and what looks like a giant black sponge.

"What's that for?"

"Cleaning the brushes. I'll show you." She turns to look out of the enormous, floor-to-ceiling window giving us a panoramic view of Altrim. "So much inspiration."

"It is beautiful." Sometimes, I still feel like I'm in a dream when I wake up and see the gushing water, the weird skimming, hovering platforms people use to travel around, the insane architecture. I shouldn't be surprised my instinct is to capture it all somehow.

I watch Deva as she adds several different dollops of paint to a palette, then picks up a brush. From what I can tell so far, the consistency of these paints seems to be closest to the oil paints we use at home. I set about adding colors to my own palette. I know exactly what I want to paint. I'm keeping it simple to start with—at least until I've learned to work with these new tools.

Deva already seems to be in the zone, that weird state of flow creatives sometimes get into when they're working. I'm bursting with questions but don't want to interrupt her. She projects an air of calm efficiency, and I like her already. Having met quite a few Ulfarri women since I first arrived here, I'm relieved I'm not entirely surrounded by overbearing Alphas.

One, as it turns out, is quite enough for me.

Pushing thoughts of Khan aside, I take a deep breath, relishing the prickle of excitement I feel as I pick up a brush and swirl the tip into the azure paint, as I saw Deva do.

Back on Earth, painting was an escape for me—one of the only things I could do that made my head actually go quiet. That made me stop overthinking. Now, I realize I'm hoping that painting here on Altrim will have the same effect.

Lord knows I could do with a little vacation from my own head right now. I spend so much time worrying about the future, about my conflicted feelings for Khan, about how they potentially want to kidnap and enslave human women —not to mention how I've been abducted and sold into slavery on an alien planet.

I'm just praying that losing myself in the creative process will help me the same way it used to.

The way the brush feels as it glides over the canvas is miraculous. Incredibly, the pigments of the paint turn even more vivid and rich as I apply them. The color is so gorgeous, it almost hurts to look at it.

Glancing up, I see how Deva cleans her brush by swirling it over the black sponge, and do the same thing with mine. It works; there's not a trace of blue left on the tip, and it's completely dry.

Amazing.

My pulse pounding, I dip my brush into some white paint, and get to work...

SIXTEEN

Emma

I LOST TRACK OF TIME. Everything ceased to exist but the way this incredible paint soaked into the canvas, the tip of my brush swirling and stroking... until I stood back and admired my handiwork.

"You have talent."

I jump at the sudden voice beside me. I'd forgotten Deva was even there. Together, we look down at what I painted: the pond at the bottom of my grandmother's garden. Home to my happiest childhood memories. I painted it from memory but looking at it now, a sudden pang of nostalgia tugs at my heart.

"Thank you," I say, remembering Deva just paid me a compliment. I look across the table to see what she painted. It's a stunning rendition of five moons, starkly purple against the midnight black, star-studded sky. Hard to say whether the day time or night time sky here is more beautiful—Ulfaria has five moons, and three suns. Astronomers from Earth would have a field day studying it all. "Your picture is gorgeous."

Deva waits until I've made eye contact, then she winks. "Ready for the magic?"

Another surge of excitement steals my breath. I was so lost in my memories, I forgot about that part. "We're going to make them move?"

"We are." She picks up the jar of what looks like finely ground flour, unscrews the lid, and glides back to her painting. "Watch." There are tiny holes in the top of the jar —like you'd have for herbs back on Earth—and she shakes it over her canvas. The powder is so fine, I can barely see it dust her painting. "Now we wait."

"How long for?" I'm as impatient as a kid on Christmas morning.

"Not long."

I join her, and stare closely at her picture. I realize I'm holding my breath.

"There." She gives a little sigh. "You see?"

At first I thought she had simply painted the stars so skillfully that it looked like they were sparkling but now I realize they really have begun to twinkle. It's subtle but so impressive.

I rub the sudden goosebumps which have appeared on my arms. "That's incredible."

"Want to do yours?"

"Yes please." We move to the other side of the table until we're standing in front of my canvas. "Can I do it, or do you have to?"

"You can try." Deva shrugs. "It may work."

I take the jar of powder from her and sniff it cautiously. It doesn't smell of anything. "I just sprinkle it over?"

"Yes. Like I did."

Again, I can't see any of the dust either leave the jar or land on the paint but I shake the jar gently until I'm sure every inch of my picture has been covered. Then I hold my breath.

I want the pond to ripple, and the leaves of the old oak tree I had so much fun climbing as a kid to move. I wonder how the dust knows what parts of the picture to animate.

"Do I need to do anything else?"

"Not a thing."

I'm holding my breath again, and let it out in a slow, careful exhale. It can't possibly be this easy. It's not going to work. Deva is some kind of witch, surely—after all, she said you had to study the craft for years.

"Maj—Emma! See? It's working!"

Sure enough, the surface of the pond is rippling gently, as if caressed by a gentle breeze. I stare at the leaves I so painstakingly drew on the tree, willing them to rustle.

When they do, I let out a delighted cry, startling Deva.

"It's working! Look! It's moving!"

"You have a great talent indeed," Deva says. "As I said, most have to study for years—"

"My Emma is special." Khan slides his arms around me from behind, nuzzling my neck.

"Look!" I'm practically bouncing in his embrace. I can't take my eyes off my painting. "Look!"

"Earth?" he asks.

"Yes. My grandparents' garden."

"Grandparents?" I can hear the puzzlement in his voice. Do they not have grandparents on Ulfaria? I realize once again how little I know about this planet and its inhabitants.

"The parents of my mother," I clarify.

"Ah."

Sudden tears sting my eyes and I blink furiously, trying to make them go away. The quiet, calm mood I was in while painting has disappeared and all my worries have come back in a rush. Khan's big hand slides down over my belly, pressing between my legs. I bite back a moan as my face heats up. Does he have to do this in front of Deva?

"Leave us," he orders the artist, as if he read my mind.

"No," I say, contradicting his order.

Deva, who had already begun packing up her materials, freezes. She stares at us both with huge eyes. I feel a wave of pity. Khan's arms have gone rigid around me. He's angry. I can feel it humming through the bond.

"I mean, would you mind leaving those things here?" I change tack. "So I can do some more painting later?"

Deva gives a little bow. "Of course, majesta." Since Khan is here, I don't correct her use of the term. "You will need more canvases."

"I will see to it that my queen has everything she needs," Khan says. "Calla will compensate you for your materials. Now go."

"Thank you so much—" I begin, but Deva speed-glides out of the room like she's being chased by hornets. "Khan. Why did you send her away?" *I was finally enjoying myself*, I want to add, but think better of it.

"It has been hours since I saw you last." His voice rumbles in his chest, against my back, and I breathe in his rich, spicy, woodsy chocolate scent. "I missed you."

He tightens his grip on my sex through my silky robes and I gasp, feeling that familiar gush his touch always elicits from my pussy. Then he slides his broad palm up until it's resting on my lower belly. I want to moan with disappointment.

"I can't wait for you to bear my heir," he says huskily. "Perhaps my seed has already taken hold."

My happiness over the painting and sudden burst of desire evaporate like wisps of smoke in the wind. "Perhaps," I say.

I hope he can't hear the anguish in my voice.

Khan

I'm starting to realize that finding a mate is all well and good—it's what comes after that which is more difficult. I spend a lot of my time in confusion. As much as I desire Emma, as much as my body craves to be near her, inside her, against her, I also find myself infuriated by her at times. And perplexed. Are all females this way, or just Hoo-man ones? Or is it just *this* one?

Living with and sharing my palace with Emma is showing me just how little time I spent with females before. Sure, I have taken my pleasure from many, but always beat a quick retreat after those interludes. And while I've always been surrounded by Ulfarri Beta females, they were there to serve me in my day to day life. Emma behaves like my equal—at least most of the time.

I wouldn't have it any other way.

It's funny how proud I was when she first stood up to me. The first couple of days after her arrival on Altrim, she was in a kind of daze—which I can understand. She was forced to deal with so many changes: a whole new world, literally, not to mention the toll estrus can take on the body. I find the rut challenging myself, even without having to get used to a whole new living situation.

But now, since she's been here for a little while, and especially since she discovered a passion for painting, she has grown more vocal about the things which please her—and especially the things that don't. She seems less intimidated by me, which is a huge relief. I don't want my mate to fear me. I want her to desire and cherish me.

Ulfarri females are taught to be graceful and calm, and that Alpha males are superior in every way.

Emma has moments where she behaves almost exactly that way.

She also has moments where she doesn't.

Still, I find it almost impossible to be angry with her. She's somehow playful in her disobedience, and a part of me enjoys sparring with her.

In any case, we both know who will win in the end.

I was unprepared for the pride I felt when I saw how talented she is at painting. At first, I had summoned Deva to indulge her—Emma was still quiet and seemed sad, and the paintings in my palace were one of the few things to arouse her interest.

I never expected my little Omega to create such stunning artwork.

Deva, too, was surprised. Beta artists spend years cultivating their talent. I got the impression Deva was a little irked by how fast Emma seemed to develop the knack, but then Emma told me how she's an artist back on Earth, and has also been training for a long time.

They just use different materials there. And apparently, their pictures don't move.

Emma is now determined to paint people. Ulfarri paint anything—food, landscapes, abstract shapes—but they have always refrained from drawing people or animals. There is a superstition that animating life forms with the magic dust is a bad omen. That giving them life on canvas will somehow cause death in the real world.

My little Omega is determined to prove everyone wrong. Years of superstition will be turned upside down if she gets her way. Deva is horrified—as are any other Betas she tells of this plan. But Emma is headstrong, and will not be deterred.

I support her in this, as I enjoy indulging her where I

can, but even I drew the line when she asked to paint me. After all, what if she's wrong?

I bade her practice on other creatures first. Insects, perhaps. Or the Stone King, she offered, which made me smile. She took an instant dislike to him, which only confirmed for me how well suited we are. I've never liked him, either.

Her rendering of him was awesome; she captured his likeness so perfectly that the painting made my skin crawl the way it does when the real king is nearby. Once she'd strewn the canvas with the magic dust, we both held our breath and waited and, sure enough, his eyes began to gleam ever so slightly from within the dark shadow of his hood.

Emma let out a little gasp. "He's so creepy," she said, stepping closer to me. I don't think she's noticed how she seeks my proximity whenever she feels unease, but I have.

In any case, the Stone King is still alive—much to our disappointment—and Deva was forced to concede that perhaps the superstition preventing Ulfarri from painting living creatures was just that: baseless superstition.

This concession was swiftly followed by joy at the thought that she and other artists can now paint animals and Ulfarri to their hearts' content.

Here for such a short time, and already my Emma is changing the planet.

I look across the table, admiring the little Omega who has so quickly become my whole world. She's so beautiful, with her golden hair cascading over her shoulders, the light from the orbs making her skin glow pale pink. She's wearing a traditional Ulfarri gown which outlines her round, delicious breasts.

Even though I am no longer in rut, my cock stiffens as I picture her naked. Is it my imagination, or are her breasts fuller than they were before? Is it too soon for her to be pregnant?

The thought of her belly growing swollen with my seed makes my chest tighten. I never knew what longing was before this Hoo-man entered my life.

"Can you pass me the pitcher?" I ask her, needing to wet my suddenly dry throat.

She looks up at me, her fork paused in mid-air on the way to her mouth. My Emma is a fussy eater. She has yet to truly enjoy any of our dishes, which is why I have the royal cook trying out all kinds of different recipes. I even had Emma describe an Earth recipe to her in an attempt to recreate a taste of her home, but since the ingredients were so different, the end result was disappointing.

"The pitcher?" Emma says, even though I know full well that she heard me.

I suppress a sigh. She's in a mood. I can feel it vibrating through our bond—defiance, and something else. Anger? Or is it frustration? "Yes. I'm thirsty."

Her huge, sky blue eyes lock onto mine as she lifts her free hand and slowly, deliberately, never breaking eye contact, pulls the pitcher even further away from me.

I give her a warning growl. "Emma."

"Yes?" She feigns innocence.

"I will not ask you again. The pitcher. Now. No!" I bark at the servant who has already begun to glide forward. She shrinks back into the shadows.

"Are you thirsty?" Emma asks. She still hasn't moved. The fork is still hovering in mid-air. "Do you want something to drink?"

What is she playing at? My fingers tighten on my thighs. Normally, I would not tolerate such insolence from a female but Emma is my mate. My queen. Her happiness is my happiness. I'm determined to find out the cause of this strange behavior before I nip it in the bud. "Yes. I do," I say, forcing my voice to remain low and calm.

"Well, *I* want a latte. I want to call my family. I want to go home. I want so many things that I'll never have again!" Her voice is shrill and rising, and her gaze is suddenly shimmering with tears. "You can just reach over and get that fucking pitcher yourself, but I don't have that option. You won't let me *have* that option! So get your own damn drink! At least you have that ability!"

Before I can reply, before I can react, there's a hideous scraping noise as she pushes the chair back and, dropping the fork with a clatter, she spins on her heel and runs out of the room.

The defiance in our bond has vanished. It's been replaced with a deep, heart-wrenching sorrow. I rub over the sudden ache in my chest, speechless.

This is the first time Emma has actually raised her voice to me in anything other than pleasure. And instead of making me angry, it makes my heart hurt.

I'm the cause of her misery, even though I have been doing everything in my power to make her happy.

I have given her the most luxurious clothing, furniture, jewels, food—I even organized an art tutor for her—and yet none of it is enough. None of it is what she really wants.

To go home.

To Earth.

There must be a solution. I will find a way to make my Emma happy. And in the meantime, I will do what I can to comfort her.

SEVENTEEN

Emma

KHAN'S RUGGED, striking face was a picture during my outburst. His lips were rounded in a perfect O, and I could sense how much he wanted to come around the table and remind me of my place. To his credit, he didn't. He sat there like a statue as I screamed at him.

Now, I'm curled up in a ball in our bed, the tears hot on my face, my eyes burning with them.

The smooth silks and plush furs are soft against my bare legs. Weirdly, that only makes me bawl harder.

Nesting, Khan calls it when I get that strange, inexplicable urge to add more and more items of comfort to our bedchamber. He allows me free rein and makes sure to indulge my every whim. If I want a silk cushion, I'm given the best silk cushion in Altrim. Purple furs. Teal rugs. Orb lamps which give off a soft, pink, flattering glow. My own paintings adorn the walls. I thought pictures of home would give me some comfort, but I was wrong. Now, the images—of my grandparents' orchard, of the white sandy beach in

Thailand, of a steaming cup of coffee—just mock me, reminding me cruelly every day of what I'm missing.

I stuff my hand against my mouth and sob louder. I've been holding it all in as much as possible ever since I arrived, distracting myself with decorating the room and painting the scenes of my happiest memories—when Khan wasn't fucking me—and now it's like a dam has broken.

My mind is racing as I weep. Now that my estrus has passed (for the time being; Khan says it will likely return in a moon's cycle at the latest), I'm able to think more clearly.

And all I can think about is my predicament—and that of the other human women they want to bring here. Just yesterday, I was told that the experiment has failed, and the Ulfarri females are unaffected by the Omega serum. In other words, Aurus the pompous twat chrome king and his magical scientists are going to start kidnapping women from Earth and bringing them to Ulfaria.

That thought is enough to bring on a fresh round of sobs. I'm hiccupping and hoarse when I hear the purring. His voice is low. Gentle. Reassuring.

"Emma. Come to me."

He joins me on the bed and I roll into his arms, still sniffling. My nose is too stuffy from crying for me to smell his scent but already the rumbling coming from his broad chest is slowing my heartbeat and soothing me.

I get a sudden craving for cookie dough ice cream, and wonder if my hormones are making me feel worse. Do Omegas get PMS?

His huge paw settles on my hip, his long, broad fingers splaying over part of my buttock. His other hand is stroking the back of my head. I don't know how he can talk while he's purring—or growling—but he can. It's like some weird kind of circular breathing.

I had expected him to be angry after my outburst. I had half expected him to bend me over and spank me, as he's done a couple times now when I've been too cheeky. Instead, he's comforting me.

I'm not sure how I feel about that.

"My sweet little thing," he croons, still stroking me. "I hate to see such sorrow."

Then let me go home! I want to bark at him, but the purring is so comforting, I don't want him to stop. I don't want to antagonize him.

Why not?

A question I cannot answer right now. Or I don't want to.

Either way, I snuggle against him instead, allowing the vibrations from his broad chest to spread through my body until my breathing is slow and deep, and the tears have dried on my face.

"I'm sorry I shouted at you," I mumble into his chest. I have to apologize. I can't help it. *You can take the girl out of England...*

To my surprise, he lets out a low chuckle. "You are the only female ever to raise her voice to me," he admits. "I would not normally tolerate such insolence for a second."

"I know." I shudder at the memory of the last time he spanked me. I can't even remember why—I may have sassed him, playfully—but he bent me over, flipped up my gown (apparently, underwear isn't a thing on this planet), and slapped my bare ass with his massive hand and brute strength until the skin felt like it had been scalded. The memory makes my clit throb, just as it did then. If Khan was surprised to find me soaking wet after he'd turned my butt the hue of ripe watermelon, he didn't show it. But I'm fairly sure he's worked out that certain kinds of pain drive me wild. Or maybe he just thought it was the estrus...

"I know what you're thinking," he continues, and I can almost feel his amusement. "But no, I will not reward such behavior. Playful defiance is one thing. Screaming at me across the dinner table—"

"Is another," I finish for him. Part of me does feel guilty. I acted like a child, and I can only imagine how he felt while I was yelling at him.

The other part of me, on the other hand, still feels justified. Every word I said was true, even if I could have expressed myself with more decorum.

His hand on my hip slides down to cup my buttock possessively, and he tugs me closer until my groin is pressed up against his crotch. His cock is rigid, huge beneath the soft fabric of his breeches.

"Let me make you feel better," he murmurs. The hand stroking my hair suddenly slides through it at the scalp, gripping it tightly, yanking my head back. And then his lips are on mine.

Even though I'm no longer in heat, my body responds to Khan. There's a sudden liquid gush between my thighs as his tongue slides into my mouth and he kisses me ferociously, expertly, on and on until my nipples are stiff, aching peaks against the gown and my clit is aching for his touch. Digging my nails into his shoulders, I moan, sliding one leg over his thigh and grinding myself against it.

He's still kissing me, his tongue plunging, foreshadowing what his cock will be doing to my pussy.

Goosebumps prickle over my skin as I gyrate my hips, the butter-soft hide of his breeches already slick with my juice. My clit feels huge as I scrape it up and down against him, riding his huge, iron thigh. As ashamed as I am for behaving like a bitch in heat, I can't stop myself.

It feels too good.

When Khan's purr turns into a growl and he bites my

lower lip, I explode, coming so hard that I see stars burst behind my closed eyelids. I'm holding on to him for dear life, shuddering violently, my core clenching uncontrollably as I cream all over his breeches.

At length I go limp, spent and exhausted, too drained to even apologize for ruining his clothing. Instead, I lie in his arms, my heart racing, tiny aftershocks still pulsing through my core.

Khan kisses my forehead with uncharacteristic tenderness. He's still growling. "My little Emma," he whispers. "Mine."

Then, like a switch has been thrown, he rolls me over, flipping me onto my back and getting astride me. My gown is unceremoniously torn open to reveal my breasts, and his mouth and fingers are on them, kneading, pinching, tugging and twisting the nipples until I cry out.

The pain just heightens my arousal.

It always has.

I don't know when or how he freed his huge, engorged cock from his breeches but as he gives my taut nipple a particularly savage bite, there's a sharp ache in my pussy and he's inside me, all the way to the hilt. Filling me. Stretching me.

My legs are splayed as obscenely around him as my sex is, and his smooth, hard pelvis is grinding against my clit with every thrust as he begins to fuck me in earnest.

"Mine," he says again, his voice thick with lust. His eyes are almost black with his desire. "Mine. Mine. Mine." He's chanting it now, in time to the exquisitely painful digs of his hips as he pounds his length into my slick core with the brutal precision I've come to know—and crave—so well. One huge hand is still gripping my breast painfully; the other is clamped across my forehead, pinning me to the mattress, nothing but a vessel for his seed.

Even though he's not actively doing anything to facilitate my pleasure, another orgasm is thundering towards me. Now that I'm not in estrus, I don't produce rivers of slick, but I'm still dripping. My juice tickles me as it slides down over my butthole. I can feel every ridge, every vein of Khan's considerable cock. Then he adjusts the angle slightly, so he's thrusting up against my G-spot as well as crushing my clit.

My entire being contracts as I clench around him, coming so hard that I don't even know where the orgasm is originating from. I just know that the pleasure is so intense, it physically hurts—an ache exacerbated when the knot forms at the base of his cock, stretching the sensitive tissue of my opening as if I were being fisted.

That only makes me come harder.

Khan lets out a roar which mingles with my scream and vaguely, I'm aware of bright spots appearing around the edges of my vision as my body milks him rhythmically.

He's filling me up, pumping me full of his cum, and as the spasms of my orgasm finally begin to wane, a feeling other than pure lust overtakes me.

Resentment, bitter as vinegar, fills me as completely as the huge Alpha on top of me is currently doing.

This is all he sees in me.

This is all he wants me for.

This is all I am to him: a cocksleeve. An empty womb to be fertilized. A broodmare.

I don't want to stay here. I don't want to lose everything I've ever known and everyone I've ever loved. I don't want to be reduced to nothing but a walking, talking set of ovaries. I don't want to have to watch as other women are kidnapped from Earth to suffer the same fate—or worse, depending on which king they're unlucky enough to be given to.

The trouble is, there's sweet fuck all I can do about any of it.

My pussy is still fluttering around Khan's cock as the tears begin, once more, to leak from my eyes.

EIGHTEEN

Khan

I'M STILL COMING down from my intense climax when I notice Emma is weeping again.

Ulf help me, I don't know what to do. I cannot bear to see her so sad, and feeling that sorrow through our bond is only making things worse.

Nor can I believe how fast she went from orgasm to tears. Her moods can change so quickly.

Still breathing heavily, trying to ignore the pounding in my loins and chest, I switch my growl back to a purr, and kiss her damp forehead. "Emma," I whisper. "Please."

I don't know what I'm asking for. I just want her to be happy. For our bond to radiate joy and lust instead of sadness and resignation.

"What, Khan?" She has stopped sobbing, which I believe is due to my purring. She blinks, and more tears leak from the corners of her huge blue eyes when she does so. But she no longer seems to be weeping. Instead, she's peering up at me, looking more directly into my eyes than she ever has. I wonder what she's hoping to see there.

"I hate to see you sad," I admit, though it pains me to talk about my feelings with anyone, let alone a female. "Tell me what you need."

Her gaze is frank. Searching. And yet I cannot decipher her thoughts. For a long moment, I hold my breath, almost drowning in her beauty. My cock is softening inside her, the slippery warmth of my seed and her slick coating the area where we're joined.

For a moment, I wonder whether today is the day when my seed will take root, then I force myself to concentrate. Now is not the time to fantasize about breeding my Omega.

"To start with, I need you to get off me," she says at length.

As I extricate myself from her and settle down by her side, I wonder whether it's her intent to humiliate me. Ulf knows that's exactly how I feel right now. Humiliated. My mate—my queen—has just given me an order, and I have obeyed.

Like a slave.

I am an Alpha. An Ulfarri. A Brutal One. I am no slave.

What is it about this little pink and golden Hoo-man that enthralls me so? I was looking for an Omega to impregnate; a female with whom to breed more Alphas and Omegas.

I was not looking to... care about her this much. And yet I do. About her sadness, her happiness, her hopes and dreams.

She matters so much to me.

This realization is such a shock that I have to force myself to redirect my attention to what she is saying. She has a sweet, soft voice, even if the translator chip does give her a strange accent when she speaks Ulfarri. It's endearing.

"...which is why I wanted more from life," she's saying. "There are enough people in the world, anyway. Well," she lets out a little huff, "on Earth, in any case. I've spent my entire life working towards breaking free from those expectations. I worked so hard in England that I was able to land a sponsored job in Virginia, for god's sake! At my age! And now I find out all that effort was for nothing. That promise to myself was for nothing—"

"What promise?" I missed the first part of what she was saying, and am struggling to follow.

She turns her head and looks at me. "The one I just mentioned. That I would never wind up barefoot and pregnant. That I would never give up my dreams just to raise kids. My mum did it, her sister, my grandmother, my sister... I wasn't going to go down that road."

Slowly, what she's saying begins to sink in. "You do not desire children?" I can't hide the incredulity from my tone.

"No! I don't! Never have, never will." She sounds so resolute. Every word is a stab in my chest.

"Females on Earth can make that choice? The males—"

"The males don't get to tell the females whether or not to reproduce, no. In fact, that side of things is usually the woman's responsibility from the get go. After all, we're the ones who go through the pregnancy, the labor, the delivery. We're the ones who do most of the childcare and, in most cases, still go out to work—either because we want to, or a single income isn't enough, or the father does a runner." She lets out a disdainful sigh.

"A runner?" The translation software is good but it isn't flawless. I'm sure she doesn't mean what I just heard.

"Yeah. They fuck off. Leave. Abandon the mother and their children."

I can hardly believe my ears. "Leave? To fight?"

Emma gives a bitter laugh. "Fight? God, no! Usually, they leave to screw someone else. Or they're bored. Or they've decided life is more fun without baby spew, dirty diapers, endless responsibility..."

"That would never happen on Ulfaria."

She raises a slim, dark golden eyebrow. "No? I mean, I can't imagine an Alpha leaving an Omega, since they're so rare, but surely Betas do it?"

I shake my head. "All offspring is precious, regardless of class. No Ulfarri male would ever abandon his family, if he is lucky enough to have one."

"Huh." She blinks, lost in thought for a moment. "I respect that."

A terrible thought occurs to me. "How do you prevent it? If you do not wish to breed?" I knew she was no virgin, but while I prefer not to think about the males who came before me, my curiosity about this particular issue is piqued.

"There are different methods. Pills. Condoms. Coils. Implants. Even operations."

"Surgical procedures? Hoo-mans undergo medical alterations to prevent pregnancy?"

"Yep. Although, most doctors won't do it unless you're either older, or you've already had a child—or three."

Sudden panic grips me in its iron fist, and my throat has constricted. "Emma..." I manage.

Another bitter laugh. "I'm only twenty-seven. No, Khan, I haven't had a hysterectomy."

I don't know what that word is, but I assume she means the sterilization procedure. "And the other methods? You use any of those?" I realize I'm holding my breath.

"I was on the pill," her tone has changed from matter-of-fact to despairing once more, "but came off it a few months ago. The hormonal methods never did agree with me."

"So—"

"Yes, Khan, that means I can have babies. But—and this is very, very important—it doesn't mean I *want* to."

It feels like there's a rock lying heavy in the pit of my stomach. I knew Emma was sad because she missed her home. Her family. Earth. It never, ever, ever occurred to me that she—any female, for that matter—would actively condemn and avoid motherhood. It's a concept as alien to me as the *caramel lattes* she sometimes mentions with a wistful look on her pretty face. "Why not?" I croak, dreading the answer.

This would all be so much easier if I could only see her as a body. A vessel to impregnate without a care for her feelings. But she is my soul mate. I cannot bear her unhappiness.

And now I discover my greatest wish is her worst nightmare.

"For all the reasons I just said!" she says impatiently. "I wanted to be free to concentrate on my career!"

"That seems selfish," I muse, almost to myself. To my absolute amazement, her small fist lands squarely on my shoulder. It doesn't hurt in the slightest, but that doesn't lessen my shock.

"So typical!" Emma has raised her voice again. The anger is livid in our bond. "Typical fucking male response! Any woman who chooses not to have kids is a selfish, dowdy, undesirable cat lady, right?"

I do not know what half of those things are, but I shake my head, taken aback by her vehemence.

"It's absolutely not selfish!" she continues, sliding off the bed and beginning to pace. The tattered ribbons of the gossamer gown I tore in my haste to get to her beautiful breasts flap around her, but she doesn't seem to even realize she's essentially naked. "There are kids dying every day of starvation! Preventable diseases! Abuse! I don't see any of the busybodies judging *me* for *my* choices lining up to take any of those children in. And until they do, they don't get to tell me I'm not a woman if I don't fucking breed!"

Her agitation is palpable. No doubt this subject is one she is very passionate about, and my first instinct—despite my shock at her confession—is, once again, to comfort her.

I must have stopped purring at some point during this conversation but I have no idea when. I take a deep breath, and start again.

Emma covers her ears with her hands. "Stop that!" she cries. "Stop fucking with me! Every time I say or do something you don't like, you purr, knowing full well it's like a sedative. *Keep her quiet so she doesn't protest*? Christ!"

For the second time in the same evening, her outburst has made me speechless. All I can do is lie on the bed, my mind reeling. "I'm not trying to silence you." I try to keep the hurt from my tone, but don't know whether I was successful. "I'm trying to comfort you."

"Well, stop it! I don't need your comfort! I just want you to *listen* to me!"

"I am listening!"

Emma takes a deep breath, lifts her chin, and comes towards me. Her honey scent tickles my nose but for once, it does not make blood rush to my groin. She perches carefully on the side of the bed. "I'm sorry. Yes, you are listening. You also asked me what I want."

I know what she's going to say, and there's a sudden band of steel around my chest.

It's hard to breathe. No wound I ever sustained in battle was this agonizing.

She says the words anyway. "Khan, I want to go back to Earth. I want a promise from you—or King Aurus—that no human women will be kidnapped and brought here to be turned into Omegas. And I don't want to breed."

It's my turn to take a deep breath. Unexpectedly,

actually hearing her speak the words has shredded the pity in my heart, and now I feel nothing but cold determination.

Sitting up, I turn to look at her fragile little face, then reach out and caress her soft cheek. I speak as slowly and deliberately as she just did. "I am Khan, the Wanderer King, ruler of Altrim, and I get what I want. All my life, I have searched for an Omega, and now I have found one. I have found a way to create more generations of Ulfarri Alphas and Omegas. I intend to begin that process with my mate. And nobody will stand in my way. Not even you."

NINETEEN

Emma

I'VE LOST track of time. I no longer know how long I've been here for—one day blends into the next, then the next. And who knows whether Ulfarri days are the same length as Earth ones?

Something in Khan snapped when I told him outright of my unwillingness to have his babies. It was almost a tangible thing, a sharp pang I felt physically. It's like there's this invisible thread connecting us, and I can feel what he feels—not as acutely, but I can sense it. He calls it *the bond*, and says he feels it too, and that we have it because we are soul mates. I hate it. My emotions are constantly muddied by his, somehow.

So when I said I don't want children, ever, the sadness was so sharp I could almost taste it. I was taken aback. I thought my views had been clear from the get go. Just because the serum forces me into estrus and I crave sex with Khan like I need air to breathe, doesn't mean I actively want the intended, ideal biological outcome. I just want the gnawing ache in my sex to be relieved.

He's been different since then. More distant. Less solicitous. He still talks to me, fucks me, purrs for me... but it's like an invisible wall has been erected. And I've been getting a lot more time to myself.

I spend most of it painting frantically, trying to quiet my mind, to get out of my own head. I paint Earth animals, birds, landscapes... but I don't dare paint anyone I care about. Even though no news has reached us telling us of the creepy Stone King's untimely demise, I don't want to risk hurting anyone else. I guess that's my own kind of superstition, since Deva has started painting every living creature they have on Ulfaria with childlike enthusiasm. The thought makes me smile. At least I've made somebody happy.

I'm putting the finishing touches to a picture of a hummingbird—as best I can remember it—when I sense Khan's presence behind me. My nostrils flare as his smokey chocolate scent fills them, and there's an instant liquid gush between my thighs.

Fuck. Being this turned on from his scent alone can only mean one thing: I'm back in estrus.

Without a word, without preamble, he shoves the hem of my dress up around my waist, bends me over, and slides his huge cock up inside me in one violent thrust.

He's growling, and even though there was no foreplay, no warning, not even a kind word, my nipples stiffen into aching points against the flimsy material of my gown, and I suppress a moan as I'm stretched, forced to accommodate his considerable girth.

He winds my hair into a fist close to the base of my skull, making my back arch, and begins to fuck me with long, deliberate thrusts.

The tingling between my legs is already intense but I'm fighting it. I've accepted the way my body responds to him, the way it overrules my mind and will, and has done since the first day I met Khan, but he made it easier because he seemed to care about my pleasure. About me.

Now, he's not even pretending anymore, and I'm furious. I don't want to give him the satisfaction of coming. Of making a single sound. Of giving the slightest hint that I'm enjoying this. I can't stop him from fucking me, especially when he's in rut, but I can control my reaction to it.

I hope.

My body seems to have other ideas. Already that familiar sensation is tightening in my core, a sure sign that I'm close to coming. While I love forced—and denied—orgasms in BDSM play, this is entirely different. I bite my lower lip, hard, to distract myself.

Khan's free hand reaches around and begins to tug my nipple through the sheer fabric of my dress.

I bite my lip harder as the pleasure shoots straight down from my breast to my groin.

Damn that fucking serum.

My last Dom used to love to deny me orgasms, keeping me on the brink for what felt like forever, threatening the worst punishments if I came without his express permission. Now I'm grateful for that practice, as I'm forced to use every bit of it.

It's working, too, until I feel Khan's warm breath on my ear and he growls a single word:

"Come."

My pussy—traitorous bitch that she is—obeys instantly, whether it's because of that weird thrall Khan has over me or because I'm a sexual submissive, I don't know. I don't really care. All that matters is that I'm exploding around his cock, coming so hard that it hurts—an exquisite, toe-curling ache—and I'm biting my lip almost all the way through in an attempt to hide my orgasm from the one who's causing it.

Bastard.

The rhythmic snatching of my pussy around his cock sets Khan off, too, and I can't hold back a yelp as his knot expands, locking me to him, ensuring I can't go anywhere as he fills me to the brim with thick, hot cum.

Just like my slick, the quantities he produces with each climax should be a physical impossibility, regardless of whether he's shooting it up inside me or covering me with it to mark me as his. It's already leaking out from around the knot and dribbling down the insides of my thighs before he's even stopped throbbing within me.

At length, the knot has softened enough that he can pull out. I hold my breath, wondering what he'll do next.

"Emma." His voice sends a shiver up my spine, and I don't resist as he turns me to face him and draws me into his embrace. His thick arms encircle me, pressing me to his massive chest, and his breath whispers over the crown of my head.

Please don't purr, I entreat him silently. I couldn't bear it.

"I want us to talk," he says. "I don't like to quarrel."

"You just rutted me like I'm some animal for you to mount," I bite out, heatedly. "And now you want to talk?"

"I'm in rut. I can't think straight when I'm hard."

The excuse used by human males since the dawn of time, I think wryly, but instead, I just let out a huff. As mad and tired as I am, his arms comfort me. They always do.

Damn it. "I don't want to talk."

"Then you can listen." Picking me up in that effortless way of his, he strides over to a nearby chaise then sits down and settles me in his lap.

The insides of my thighs are sticky with dried cum and

girl juice. *Baby batter*, I think irrationally, and suddenly have to fight the urge to weep.

"I want you to know why it is so important for me to breed," he goes on.

"I don't care," I mutter.

"I don't believe that."

"I don't care what you believe." Now I sound petulant, but fuck it. I'm tired of feeling powerless. Handing over control of some aspects of my life to a trustworthy Dom within agreed, established boundaries and with a safeword is one thing. This is quite another. I'm not in control of *anything*. Where I live. Where I go. Whom I associate with. What I eat. What I wear. When I have sex, for fuck's sake. And now I have to talk when all I want to do is get back to my painting.

Khan's grip tightens around me, as if he heard my thoughts and wants to confirm them. God, this is all so unfair.

"There's still so much you don't know about Ulfaria," he begins. "And you will learn, in time, but one of the most important aspects is our history. Ulfarri are a warrior species. This planet is rich in resources, and others have tried to conquer it—conquer *us*—since the beginning of time. To preserve our way of life, our planet, to protect the Betas—Ulf, to *survive*—we've had to maintain a big enough army of Alpha soldiers. That army is now dwindling."

I think back to the rows and rows of golden-headed Alphas standing outside the Golden Palace, and give a snort. "Didn't look like it to me when we arrived."

"The ones you saw are the last generation. Alphas are so rarely born to Beta/Beta pairings that, if attacked, we will no longer have adequate defenses in a few suns' time—unless we manage to replenish the armies we have now. We need Alpha babies. Lots and lots of them. And for that, we need Omegas."

I'm silent for a moment, absorbing his words. It makes sense. But I still don't see why I should be the one to bear all that responsibility. Nor could I birth an entire Alpha army even if I were the most baby-mad woman in the world.

"As well as breeding strong Alphas, Omegas have other qualities which are sorely lacking from Altrim—and Ulfaria—since they essentially died out."

"Such as?" I can't help asking.

"They are gentle. Kind. Nurturing. They are able to soothe and calm Alphas in ways no Betas can."

"By spreading their legs?" I scoff.

If Khan is getting impatient with my attitude, he's not showing it. I have to admire him for that. "While it is true that only Omegas can induce the rut—and slake it, to a tiny degree," he gives a rueful smile, "that wasn't what I meant. Beta females can't calm Alphas the way Omegas can."

I think about the way I react whenever he purrs to me. How soothing it is. Better than any Valium, oil massage, bubble bath. "How?"

"They hum. My mother used to sing to me. Lullabies."

He's never spoken about his parents—or his family in general. I didn't ask. I figured he'd tell me if he wanted to. I remain silent, listening.

"My mother was one of the last Omegas." Now he sounds wistful, almost melancholy. I've never seen this side of him before. It's bizarre to watch this huge warrior wear an expression like a little boy's. He almost sounds like one, too. A sudden unexpected mental image of a little boy in his likeness—our son—flashes in my mind's eye. I quickly quash it. "She birthed me late, after many, many attempts. Many failed pregnancies."

I feel a pang of empathy. Losing a child is one of the

most terrible things a woman can go through—even I know that. And to be an Omega, with so much importance placed on breeding—the pressure must have exacerbated the grief... I can't imagine going through that once, let alone several times. "I assume your father was an Alpha?"

"Of course. Beta males can't breed with Omegas. So yes, my father was an Alpha. One of the finest." The pride in his tone is unmistakable. "He was slain defending Altrim from a particularly fierce race we call the Chitin. I was barely grown, but at least I was no longer a child when that happened."

"And your mother?" I'm almost afraid to ask.

"Sickness took her when I was still young. I had barely reached maturity when I had to assume the role of king."

So much burden to put on young shoulders—even if they were broad, Alpha shoulders. I can't help reaching out to stroke his cheek. His midnight stubble is rough beneath the pads of my fingers. He looks down at me, and his eyes are filled with tenderness. "I'm sorry," I whisper.

He catches my hand and holds it gently. "Kind, compassionate, and gentle: a true Omega," he murmurs. "And I don't believe that was caused by the serum. I believe you were always that way. Always had those traits."

"They're not really rare traits, where I come from," I say. "I mean, there are selfish, unfeeling assholes, too, but I'd say it's a fairly even split."

"Be that as it may. You're special, Emma. I see some aspects of my mother in you."

Not exactly a line most women want to hear, but I know how he means it, and I'm more touched than I'd like to admit. "Thank you." There's a sudden lump in my throat. Maybe he does care. Maybe he is more capable of feeling than I suspected at first.

But that doesn't negate the fact that I'm not here of my

own free will. Nothing, no kind words, good sex, or purring will change that. Ever.

Khan

Emma sleeps curled into herself. She's thinner; she's barely been eating, claiming she cannot easily stomach Ulfarri food. She is distressed and anxious. Not even painting seems to interest her much anymore. Her unhappiness throbs in our bond. I hold her until she falls asleep, but then I rise, restless.

Even after our conversation the other day, where I thought I'd made it clear to her how important Omegas are to our very survival, she says she will not, cannot, accept her life here.

And so I find myself poised on a stool in my private quarters, in a room closed off from Emma but close enough that I can hear her cries. Her distress is always with me, a dull ache in my heart. It cannot go on.

There is only one solution.

I sit with muscles rigid and tense until the orb in front of me flares with a golden light. It's King Aurus, answering my hail.

"Khan?" Aurus rumbles. He sounds surprised.

"Aurus. I need a favor," I say roughly.

There's a pause. Aurus knows me well. I do not easily ask for help. Aurus would consider doing so a weakness; an Alpha would never willingly show weakness to a rival. And all kings are rivals, even as we are allies. The truce between us is an uneasy one.

"Ask." Aurus makes it sound like an order. But he can't help himself.

"I want your magicians to create a portal so I can return my Omega to her home planet."

"Return your Omega?" Disbelief tinges his tone. "Does she not please you?"

"She wishes to return home," I say simply.

There's a longer pause. "I will order my magicians to look into it," he says. "They are attempting to create a portal to summon Hoo-mans. Returning one is surely possible."

It is the answer I need—and hate to hear. "Thank you."

Aurus doesn't seem to know what to say to that. I sit in silence, poised on my stool, waiting for him to think through the questions he wants to ask. He needs to know why I would relinquish my Emma.

"The other kings will not like it if you obtain a second Omega before they do," he says at length.

"There is no need for jealousy. I will not take a second Omega."

"No?" To Aurus and any other king, this notion is inconceivable.

"No." Emma is the only one for me. I can hardly believe it even as the words leave my lips but it's the truth. She is my soul mate. I desire her more than anything else—even more than I desire an heir.

There's another long silence. For once, Aurus is speechless. It took an Omega and a king's sacrifice to do it.

"You have given us a great gift," he says finally in rolling, regal tones. He cannot see my small smile. Out of all the kings, I am the one who found Omegas for our planet. Perhaps it is because I was born to one. My mother was in the last generation of her kind.

Now, Alphas are born in rare instances of Beta/Beta pairings. Aurus was born to such a couple, and taken from his home at a young age to live and rise among the ranks of the Alpha soldiers. He has never known the tenderness of an Omega mother like I have.

I still remember my mother's scent. I hear her humming songs late at night. Perhaps that is why I never stopped hunting for what our planet has lost.

And now that I've found Emma, I must give her up. Her life is my life. Her happiness is my happiness.

"I hope I will come to possess an Omega as beautiful as yours."

He thinks he will possess his Omega, when truly she will possess him. She will turn his life upside down. I cannot wait.

"Emma is beautiful. She is also headstrong. She is upset we are taking more Hoo-man females," I offer.

"It cannot be helped," Aurus says, his tone turning grim. "If the Alphas die out..."

"I know." I do understand. The survival of our planet depends on our greatest, strongest dynamic. And with Beta/Beta only pairings, Alphas will become even more rare.

I cannot stop more Hoo-man women from being taken. But I will do all I can to see my Omega happy. Even if that means giving up all I ever wanted.

TWENTY

Emma

WE'RE BACK on Khan's spaceship. Khan is quiet. I'm sitting in his lap because he refuses to let go of me.

I didn't ask what was happening when he bundled me into his arms and carried me from the nest. I didn't care. My head is throbbing like tiny ice picks are being shoved into my temples, and my mouth is dry. Maybe it's the estrus. I feel like I've been in one since I met Khan. Maybe I have, although Khan swears they only last a few days at a time. Or maybe I'm still adjusting to the planet. The new environment. My fucked up new life.

Not all of it is fucked up, though. Altrim is beautiful. And Khan is... complicated. I peek at him from the corner of my eye. His features are composed, somber. Almost thoughtful. The bond between us is like a lead weight, radiating pain. It wasn't like that a day ago. The ache has grown in the past few hours, filling our connection until I'm afraid to probe it. Like a rotting tooth.

I resist the urge to rub my chest or look at Khan any longer. Instead, I stare out of the large window. For most of the journey, the scenery has flashed by but as the ship slows, I realize the landscape has a familiar golden glimmer.

A shot of trepidation makes me shift on Khan's lap.

"Did Aurus call another Kings' Council? Is that where we're going?" I break the silence. My hands are rigid in my lap, my nails biting into my palms. I don't want to sit through another horrible meeting where the Alpha kings discuss the fate of human women.

Khan strokes my hair. He senses my nerves but isn't purring. That alone puts me even more on edge. But maybe he's just heeding my plea to stop purring every time I'm distressed.

"No. There's no council meeting," he says simply.

Then why are we returning to the Golden Palace? Aurus's gaudy place glimmers in the distance. The suns are setting but in the low light, the gold and white structure is no less breathtaking. This time, there are no lines of Alpha soldiers on the golden road. There's no sign of anyone at all. Rising high in the sky is the cluster of five moons, the half outline of each one fainter than the last.

The ship sails up to the Golden Palace and hovers near the steps. Outside, the evening air still holds the heat, but there are no sounds like birds or any living thing. The place is opulent as a picture, and silent as a tomb.

Khan carries me out of the ship and into the palace. My sense of dread grows as he strides down the silent halls between the giant columns. Glowing orbs hang in the air between each set of pillars, lighting our way.

I have another terrifying thought: he didn't rut me before we came here. Didn't mark me with his scent. Why not? Is he not worried about another Alpha taking me, like he was before?

We head back via the same route to the same set of doors leading to the council room—or one identical to it. His steps slow and falter a moment but then the doors open slowly, automatically.

This room has no round table and no chairs. There are a few glowing orbs in the corner but they show mostly robed Betas. I recognize Betas more easily now—they're smaller in stature. The chief Beta has purple robes, long, spidery fingers, and a bald head. He's standing in front of a giant mirror-looking thing in a golden frame. Instead of glass there's a milky white substance, like fog, moving and forming a thick wall between the gilt sides.

Khan strides in and stands before the creepy mirror thing. The head Beta and all the rest bow low.

"Wanderer King."

Khan doesn't acknowledge them, or put me down.

"Khan." Aurus enters, as big and broad as I remember him. His hair is shorn short, and he looks like a fancy gladiator in his armored chest plate. He bows his head solemnly, more respectful than I've ever seen him. "King-Who-Found-the-Omegas." He says it like a title. That's new. Then he turns to me. "Omega." He bows a little bit more deeply.

"What have you found?" Khan says, sounding impatient. My Alpha doesn't stand on ceremony. Which I prefer. *My Alpha.* Funny how much has changed. How quickly I'm thinking of Khan as mine. I'm glad I ended up with Khan instead of Aurus. Or another—like the Stone King. *Shudder.*

Aurus nods to the purple-robed magician, who steps up and clears his throat. I grilled Khan about the magicians but never got a straight answer. He doesn't seem too bothered with the details of what they do. Magicians seem to be something like a cross between scientists and engineers. But their tech is like magic to the Ulfarri.

"We have calculated the position of Earth related to the

moons," the bald-headed magician says in a surprisingly deep voice. "Very soon, they will be aligned."

"The portal will allow passage through to Earth," Aurus says.

The purple-robed magician adds, redundantly, "Your Omega's home planet."

I stiffen in Khan's arms. *Earth.* Are they talking about bringing human women through? I knew it was bound to happen but I didn't want to have to watch.

I start to struggle, and Khan clamps his arms tighter around me.

"Travel through the portal will work both ways?" he asks.

"Yes," the head Beta says. "She will return much the way she came."

"Wait," I say, loudly enough that my voice echoes in the low lit room. "Return?" Does this mean I can go back?

Khan sets me down and turns me to face him. The somber look on his features has a sort of sadness to it. I was right, then. "Do you still wish to return to Earth?"

The answer sticks in my throat. Of course I want to go back? Don't I?

"Are you serious?" *There's a portal. The impossible has happened. That's good news... right?* I lick my dry lips. "I can go back?"

Khan nods slowly. "If that is what you wish—"

"The portal will only work for a brief moment," the Beta interrupts. "It will soon be ready. As the moons align." As he speaks, the fog moves rapidly within the golden frame. There's a flurry of activity as the Betas in their robes rush around. A few are carrying tablets, and the others group themselves around the tablet-holders, pointing and nodding, or shaking their heads.

They've figured out a way back to Earth. I can go back.

Back to my old life. My MacBook Air and iPhone. My work desk, with drawing pencils I rarely use locked in the drawer. Netflix. Normalcy. Everything will be as it was.

"What about the serum?" Khan asks the Beta. He sounds very calm. It's good he's thinking up all these questions. I'm still trying to get my mind wrapped around what's happening. I wish he'd given me some kind of warning.

"The serum should go dormant. We must take a blood sample to be sure." The Beta bows his head to Khan. "With your permission?" It's annoying how the Beta asks Khan and not me.

Khan nods his permission and I pointedly add, "That's okay," and hold out my arm for a silent servant to approach and set some sort of silvery tube against my bicep. There's no pain, just a whooshing sound, and then the Beta whisks the tube away, hurrying to the corner and more fancy silver equipment that must be some sort of portable blood lab.

I can go back. Caramel lattes, and chocolate, and Taco Tuesdays with my friends. Not that I have many friends in the States yet—most of the people I know are at my job. I could try the club again...

But what about Khan?

I'll be there, and Khan will be left here. *Khan...* Automatically, I reach for him. He takes my hand and holds it loosely as Betas scurry to and fro, taking care not to get too close to the portal. The head magician is the only one standing near it, and even he is a few feet away.

"Soon. You must be ready," the head magician says, and motions me forward.

"Okay. I'll be ready," I say, a bit breathlessly. My chest is tight as I take a few steps to square up to the portal. The fog has solidified into a dull silvery substance that looks like mercury. Still creepy as hell, but supposedly it leads back home.

Home. Back to hot cocoa, and traffic on I-95. Back to paperwork to keep my green card status, and blocking my awful family on Facebook. Back to my monotonous job and my dingy apartment.

Wait a minute...

The portal is growing brighter, now it's a pale silvery blue. It shimmers like water—or a hypnotic metallic veil. There are shapes moving beyond it. I take a step forward, and halt. Am I really going to go through that thing?

"Is it safe?" Khan asks. "Is the portal safe for a human to go through?"

"Yes," the head magician says. A subordinate rushes up to him with a tablet, and he peers at it. "Yes, it's safe for a human. There's a high percentage of her surviving."

Ack. That doesn't sound good. But this is my chance to go back... can I refuse? Do I want to?

I bite my lip. No more palace in the mountains. No more moving paintings. No more estrus. I'll have to trot around to clubs, or try online dating to get my needs met.

No more Khan.

I squeeze his fingers.

"And what about for me?" Khan asks. "What is my survival rate?"

The head magician frowns at his tablet. Stunned, I try to drop Khan's hand, but he won't let me. He grips me more firmly, threading his fingers with mine.

"Khan?" My voice is raspy as I turn to him, my throat suddenly constricted. His scent blankets me.

"I will not leave you," he growls. "Do not ask me to." With his free hand, he strokes my cheek. "There is nothing here in Ulfaria for me. Without you, there is nothing."

There's a flash of light. The portal's bright with a white blue glare. It's like looking into a floodlight.

"Soon," the Beta calls. "There is a slim chance of an Ulfarri surviving travel through the portal."

"But your people? Your kingdom?" I bleat. My heart is pounding. This is all happening so fast, and I feel rushed. Pressured. Panicky.

"I will leave another in charge."

I glance at Aurus. "And the other humans? The women?"

Khan grasps my chin and pulls my gaze to his. "The human females will be acquired one way or another. I cannot stop that. But I can give this to you."

The head Beta looks up from his tablet and announces, "Survival rate for the human is ninety-five point two percent. Are you prepared to accept this risk?"

"Yes," I say, because I don't have any idea but I don't want to say no to my options. Ninety-five percent isn't bad. It isn't perfect, but...

The Beta turns to Khan. "Survival rate for an Ulfarri is twenty point nine percent."

"What?" I grimace as a cold prickle of fear creeps up the back of my neck. That's less than a quarter! "No!"

Khan growls and grips my hand. "Emma—"

"I do not advise you to travel through the portal," the head Beta continues. There's not a great bedside manner in his matter-of-fact tone. "The air will be hard on you. If you do choose to go, and survive the trip, you must find medical care immediately upon your arrival on the other side. Do you understand?"

"I understand," Khan says. Still so calm. Beneath the sorrow I feel vibrating in our bond, I detect something else. Resignation. It's about to break my heart.

"The portal is almost ready." The head magician hands

off his tablet. He steps to the side and gestures like a solemn, priestly Vanna White. "The moons are in place, and it will soon be time."

"Wait, no." I raise a hand to block out the pulsing light. "You can't come. I don't have medical care." I'm pretty sure my health insurance won't cover him. Even if Khan's anatomy is similar to a human's, they would put them in a lab and study him. "What if I can't get him medical help in time?" I ask. My heart is crashing against my ribs now; it's hard to breathe.

"Then he will die," the magician says in a flat tone as if he's totally bored by the conversation. Not much empathy required for the position of head magician, apparently.

The light flares.

"The portal is ready. You have one minute."

Khan steps to my side, still holding my hand. "Are you ready?"

"No! Khan, you have to stay here! You can't come with me." I try to twist away, but his grip is like iron. No escape. If I go, he'll be coming with me. I can't stop him.

The portal is a giant rectangle of rippling light. On the other side is my home—if the Beta magicians can be trusted and believed.

Home, where there's one sun. One moon. And taxes. And bounced checks. And rent. And stupid bosses...

And Khan. He'll step through the portal with me and venture into an alien land. Just like that. I'll watch him make the ultimate sacrifice for me. Give up everything he's ever known. For me.

And then I'll watch him die.

"Thirty seconds," the Beta intones. I taste blood. A pinching sensation in my lip. I've bitten myself. There's a physical ache humming in our bond, and I can't tell whether it's Khan's pain, or mine.

"Emma." Khan brushes my cheek with his thumb. "It is time." And he ushers me forward a little bit. My steps slow as we get closer to the portal, my legs getting heavier and heavier. My body remembers this. My mind flashes over everything that's happened—getting sucked into a bog, waking up in a cage. The auction house and the barnyard of smells. Khan roaring in the background, and my body responding.

My skin tingles, and I break out in a sweat. No more Khan. No more purring. No more rutting. No more love. A life of freedom bleak and empty as a desert stretches before me. And I don't want it anymore. I choose the cage.

I whirl around and, with my free hand, I grab Khan's muscled arm, gripping it tight.

"No," I say. My palm is slick and clammy and my grip slips a little. "No. Stop."

"Ten seconds," the Beta says.

"The portal is closing," Aurus thunders behind us.

But I pull Khan back. "I don't want this." I dig my nails into his muscles; his smoky chocolate scent filling my nostrils. The thought of never smelling it again is almost my undoing. "I don't want to live without you!"

"Emma—" Khan's face and torso are caught in the flare, his violet skin paling, making his dark tattoos stand out in stark relief. The pressure of the air chokes me. My blood is roaring in my ears. Did the portal open up and swallow us? Did we fall in? We might be dying. This might be the last moment of my life, and I need to make sure Khan knows.

"You," I shout as the portal light floods around us, blinding me, making the Alpha before me vanish. "I choose you!" The brightness is so thick, it buoys up my body. I can still feel Khan and clutch him, swimming in air. A roaring rush of wind crushes my ears, every cell in me stands up and screams, and then the world goes dark.

TWENTY-ONE

Emma

"EMMA, EMMA," a deep voice is softly calling. It's Khan. I'm in his lap. His scent is chocolate, and pine, and a campfire out under the endless stars.

"Khan?" I squint, trying to see but my eyes are burning a little, like I looked at the sun for too long. "What happened?"

"You passed out."

"Where am I?"

"Altrim. Back at my palace." A soft damp cloth touches my forehead and cheeks gently before Khan pulls it away. "The portal closed. There was nothing we could do. So I brought you here."

"Are you okay?" I ask. I crack my eyes open a little more. I need to see him. Calm is vibrating through the bond, soothing me, but I still need to see my Alpha. I need the reassurance.

"Yes, little Omega." There's an amused crinkle in the corner of his mouth. "I am well because you're safe."

"Are we home?" My voice cracks on the last word.

A crease appears in his brow before it smoothes away. "Yes, Emma." He caresses my cheek. "We are home."

"You were going to go with me..." I trail off, trying to comprehend the enormity of the last few hours. Khan was prepared to give everything up for me. He'd spent his entire life searching for an Omega with whom to start a family, and then he found me... and yet...

"I was." His rugged face is wreathed in smiles but there are dark circles beneath his hooded, glittering eyes. "I told you, nothing here has meaning without you."

"You could have died." The realization actually hits me then, and I choke back a sob.

"A risk I was willing to take." He reaches out and brushes away the tear sliding down my cheek. "You are my mate, Emma. My soul mate. We only find one in a lifetime —most don't even find that. Many don't even believe a soul bond exists, but when I found you, I knew."

"And your heirs? What about the need to replenish the Alpha army?"

He gives me a wry grin. "I wasn't expecting you to birth an entire army, anyway," he says. "Now we have found a way to obtain Omegas, the other kings will be able to ensure the survival of our race with them. They will have Alpha and Omega babies who, in turn, will grow up to make more. And so on."

"You really were prepared to make that sacrifice. For me..." I'm talking to myself more than asking him a direct question. I already know the answer. He proved it.

And I feel like my heart might explode. I didn't realize I love him—genuinely love him—until the magician said he might die going through the portal.

"Khan..." I begin. He needs to know. "When that Beta said you only had a twenty percent chance of survival, I realized something."

"What was that?" There's infinite tenderness in his eyes, as well as something else. A knowing gleam.

"I love you." I look away, suddenly shy. "And I had another crazy thought..." *Can I tell him?* I barely wanted to admit it to myself.

"Yes?" he prompts, when I trail off.

I take a deep breath. "I kind of wished I was pregnant, so I'd at least still have a part of you when you were gone."

Khan's reaction surprises me. Instead of displaying shock or delight, he merely raises an eyebrow. "Is that so?"

I nod.

Reaching out, he takes my hand, squeezing it. "There's something I have to tell you now," he says, "and it might distress you. Would you like me to purr?"

My heart starts to pound, and I feel the first prickles of panic. "No. Just tell me."

"You're pregnant," he says, and to his credit, he doesn't look at all smug. Just apprehensive as hell.

I can hardly believe my ears. "How do you know?" I croak.

"You passed out before we could go through the portal. I had the magicians look you over. I thought it was just because estrus is hard on Omegas—and it might be even harder on human females. You weren't eating, had lost weight, and were tired all the time..."

I already knew he'd noticed that, but only now do I realize that all along, the signs of how much he cares about me were there. I was just too homesick and caught up in my own misery to see them.

"I'm pregnant?" Instinctively, I put a hand to my belly. "Oh, god."

"I'm so sorry, Emma." He looks genuinely upset. "As much as I wanted this, now that I know how much you don't..." He trails off.

I study his striking, familiar face—the one I've seen contorted in anger, lust, and ice-cold brutality as he hacked through those aliens at the auction. Carefully, I probe my feelings about what he's just told me. I'm not nearly as freaked out as I thought I would be.

"It's okay," I tell him. "I'm not mad. In fact, the more I think about it, the more I'm coming to realize that I'm actually excited." As I say it, I realize it's the truth. Just because I'm going to have a baby that doesn't mean I have to give up my other love: painting. I won't be barefoot and pregnant to a deadbeat dad who treats me like crap—if he even sticks around. I won't have to sacrifice my career to raise a kid. *That* was what I was really afraid of. Not actually having children.

"Really?" His face lights up with sudden, sheer happiness. It's like a lamp has been switched on within him. "You're excited?"

"I am." It's the truth. Not only do I get to be with my mate—who loves me so much he'd actually die for me, for fuck's sake—but I get to give him his greatest wish. His heart's desire.

An image of a mini-Khan flashes in my mind. Or maybe it will be a little girl. Will she have my skin, or his? Whose eyes? Will she have the Ulfarri tattoo markings? Then I panic. "But can we even... I mean, will it be viable?" I'm using the most clinical term I can think of to distance myself from the awful thought that maybe our genes just aren't compatible.

"The magicians assure me that you will carry a healthy baby to term—or at least, you have as great a chance of that as any other human or Ulfarri female of fertile age." The jagged sorrow flashes across his face as quick as lightning, but I still catch it, and know he's thinking about his mother.

"You just need to take care of yourself. I need to take care of you."

"You already do," I say, squeezing his hand.

"I love you, little Emma," he says, and even though I already knew how he felt about me, hearing him actually speak the words brings more tears to my eyes. Tears of joy.

"I love you too," I manage.

Leaning over, he kisses me, not with the usual ferocity and savage lust, but with a tenderness that makes my heart ache. "Now sleep," he says, stroking his hand over my eyes to make me close them. "You are safe. You are home. And I am here."

I inhale deeply, breathing in his smokey pine scent.

Khan begins to purr.

EPILOGUE

Emma

Sunset is a magical time in my painting studio. Light streams into my quiet corner of the palace, making the air shimmer. The magic hour. The perfect end to my painting session—and day.

I take a few steps and dip my feet into the cool water running its course through the carved channel. The stream flows to an infinity pool at the edge of the large platform, and falls to crash on a platform below. Beyond the infinity pool, the sky is lavender, fading to a bluish purple at the corner of the horizon.

I stretch, loosening my taut muscles. I've been painting in my studio for hours but it feels like the blink of an eye. I wouldn't notice the time passing but for the suns' setting, and the heaviness in my breasts.

There's a tiny cry, and my milk lets down, making me bite my lip. I whirl as a stone section of the wall moves aside and creates a doorway. Khan steps through, holding a tiny blanketed bundle.

Our daughter.

My mate swiftly walks the length of the giant room, passing the canvases I've leaned against the towering walls.

"I stayed away as long as I could," he says, apology in his tone. "But now she wants you."

I scoot back so I can sit in my comfiest chair and unclasp the brooch at the top of my gown. The fabric falls away, baring my breasts. Ulfarri clothing is very comfortable and well designed, especially for lactating Omegas.

By the time Khan reaches me, I'm ready to nurse my daughter. I hold out my arms for her. He sets our little one in my arms, and something in me sighs. The last catch of tension in my shoulders melts away.

"There you are," I murmur, loosening my baby's midnight blue blanket so she can turn her head and find my nipple. Her tiny face scrunches up, then relaxes as the milk flows. Her little fist rests on the curve of my breast.

Our daughter's skin is a very pale shade of lavender—like the section of sky closest to the brightest Ulfarri suns. Her hair is light blue. The color of Earth's sky. Earth and Ulfaria melded together—that's Emilia. The best of Khan and myself.

I shift her to my left breast and she whimpers. "Hush, little one," I say. "All will be well."

My mate hovers over both of us, his towering height casting a shadow over our faces. His guarded silence makes me feel safe. Khan rarely leaves my side, except to let me paint.

"Mommy was painting you," I murmur to our daughter, then nod to Khan. "Take a look. I've done another portrait."

He turns the canvas so we both can study it. The three of us are hovering on a skimmer above a silvery lake. Behind us, I painted the Altrim mountains rising in the distance, the regal expanse done in thick slashes of brown and green. Khan and I are smiling, and our clothing flutters in an invisible breeze.

"This is different than the last," Khan says. His brow furrows, and he cocks his head to the side.

"Right." I duck my head and hide a smile against Emilia's head. Khan's expanding his knowledge about art. The last few paintings I did were of us sitting in a garden. Those were light and airy, like a Mary Cassatt. The alien colors of my new world added a touch of whimsy.

"I like it." He gives the canvas a nod, and returns to my side. "It has a sense of..."

"Grandeur."

"Yes. Well done." He catches my smirk, and touches my cheek. He takes time to study and murmur his approval of all my paintings, but once he got over that weird superstition Ulfarri have about animating living beings, he was obviously delighted when I began to paint him. It must be an Alpha thing. Their egos could power the suns.

Aurus had better never find out I paint portraits. He'd be begging for a life-sized one of himself. Or a giant one he can hang on a wall of his palace. I'd have to make it a hundred times his size before he'd be satisfied.

Not that we've heard much from Aurus lately. He's too busy with his Omega.

My daughter's mouth slackens on my breast. She pulls off with a sigh, and gives an adorable little burp.

"There now," I murmur. "Did Daddy wear you out?" Emilia's eyes flutter shut.

Khan takes her, and strolls back to our bedroom, patting the baby's back. I follow him out of my studio, and into our cavernous chambers. Emilia is asleep before Khan reaches her crib.

"We have a few hours," he says, swaddling her tight

and laying her down. Her pale lilac face peeks out of the midnight blue blanket. Little baby burrito.

Khan turns, his broad shoulders blocking my view. The heat in his dark eyes halts my steps, sending a shot of arousal through my core. His scent surrounds me, and already I can feel the slick leaking down my inner thighs.

A few strides, and he's scooped me up against his hard chest. "Are you tired?" he murmurs.

"No." I wind my arms around his neck, ducking my head close to inhale his musk. His blue-black hair fans across my face. His scent is cinnamony today, deepening into the mouthwatering richness of his usual chocolate smell.

"Are you hungry?" Still carrying me, he leaves our daughter's bedroom and heads to a table covered in food. "Thirsty?"

"No." My voice is low and husky. I thread my fingers deeper in his dark hair so my nails can scratch lightly at his scalp.

Khan switches directions, heading toward our bedroom. Our nest. His growl starts to rumble through me and my body responds, my clit pulsing. I twist in his arms, angling my body so I'm pressed against him. My flowy gown bunches around my hips as he lets me straddle him. And then we're down on the bed. He's on top, of course, his weighted bulk covering me. Strong hands grasp my wrists, pinning them above my head.

"My Emma," he purrs. "Mine."

"Yours," I breathe, just before his lips come crashing down over mine.

WANT MORE OMEGAVERSE? One click ***Brutal Claim*** *now!*

. . .

CLICK HERE to read the first two chapters of Kim & Alpha King Aurus' book.

Brutal Claim

Book 2 in the Planet of Kings Series

Aurus:

The High King of Ulfaria needs no introduction. What I need is an Omega.

And now, I've found one. Kim. She is small and perfect, as I knew she would be.

I will demand her obedience, then I will give her the perfect nest and allow her to bear my heirs.

She vows to defy me, but one way or another, she will submit.

Kim:

Hold. My. Beer.

ABOUT TABITHA BLACK

USA Today bestselling author Tabitha Black has been writing kinky romance for over fifteen years. While her first books were historical, she then discovered the joys of writing more contemporary books with a greater emphasis on BDSM, as well as darker, edgier fiction. Her latest forays are into dark paranormal romance, including the fascinating world of M/f Omegaverse.

She has a weakness for great coffee, strong, dominant men, and tattoos.

Tabitha loves getting mail, so if you want to drop her a line, please do so at tabitha_black@hotmail.com. You can also sign up for her newsletter, follow her on BookBub, or join her Facebook page. Thank you for reading!

Don't miss these other exciting books by Tabitha Black!

Contemporary

His Empire Series
Restraint - Book 1
Denial - Book 2
Anticipation - Novella

Masters of the Castle Series
Fulfilling Her Fantasy
Sharing Silver
Tempting Tasha

Undoing Una

Midnight Doms
Her Vampire Addiction

Anthologies
When the Gavel Falls (Sharing Silver)
Witness Protection Program (Tempting Tasha)
Dominating His Valentine (Anticipation)
Daddies of the Castle (Undoing Una)

Paranormal

Alphas of Sandor
Primal Possession - Book 1
Primal Mate - Book 2

Planet of Kings - With Lee Savino
Brutal Mate - Book 1
Brutal Claim - Book 2 (available Oct 2021)

Audiobooks

Little Tudor Rose
Conquering Cassia
Restraint
Sapphire's Surrender
Primal Possession

ABOUT LEE SAVINO

Lee Savino is a USA today bestselling author of smexy romance. Smexy, as in "smart and sexy." Find her in the Goddess Group on facebook and download a free book at www.leesavino.com!

Find her at:
www.leesavino.com

Want more growly alphas? Check out the Berserker Saga. Start with Sold to the Berserkers.

Remember to download your free book at www.leesavino.com

The Berserker Saga

Sold to the Berserkers – Brenna, Samuel & Daegan
Mated to the Berserkers - – Brenna, Samuel & Daegan
Bred by the Berserkers (FREE novella only available at www.leesavino.com) - – Brenna, Samuel & Daegan
Taken by the Berserkers – Sabine, Ragnvald & Maddox
Given to the Berserkers – Muriel and her mates
Claimed by the Berserkers – Fleur and her mates

Ménage Sci Fi Romance

Draekons (Dragons in Exile) with Lili Zander (ménage alien dragons)

Crashed spaceship. Prison planet. Two big, hulking, bronzed aliens who turn into dragons. The best part? The dragons insist I'm their mate.

Paranormal romance

Bad Boy Alphas with Renee Rose (bad boy werewolves)
Never ever date a werewolf.

Possessive Warrior Sci fi romance

Draekon Rebel Force with Lili Zander
Start with Draekon Warrior

Tsenturion Warriors with Golden Angel
Start with Alien Captive

Contemporary Romance

Royal Bad Boy
I'm not falling in love with my arrogant, annoying, sex god boss. Nope. No way.

Royally Fake Fiancé
The Duke of New Arcadia has an image problem only a fiancé can fix. And I'm the lucky lady he's chosen to play Cinderella.

Beauty & The Lumberjacks
After this logging season, I'm giving up sex. For...reasons.

Her Marine Daddy
My hot Marine hero wants me to call him daddy…

Her Dueling Daddies
Two daddies are better than one.

Innocence: dark mafia romance with Stasia Black
I'm the king of the criminal underworld. I always get what I want. And she is my obsession.

Beauty's Beast: a dark romance with Stasia Black
Years ago, Daphne's father stole from me. Now it's time for her to pay her family's debt…with her body.

Printed in Poland
by Amazon Fulfillment
Poland Sp. z o.o., Wrocław